SAFE
HARBOUR

SAFE HARBOUR

CHRISTINA KILBOURNE

DUNDURN
TORONTO

Publisher: Scott Fraser | Acquiring editor: Kathryn Lane | Editor: Shannon Whibbs
Cover designer: Laura Boyle
Cover image: Tent © istock.com/Adventure_Photo, skyline © istock.com/lvcandy
Printer: Webcom, a division of Marquis Book Printing Inc.

Library and Archives Canada Cataloguing in Publication

Title: Safe harbour / Christina Kilbourne
Names: Kilbourne, Christina, 1967- author.
Identifiers: Canadiana (print) 20190081112 | Canadiana (ebook) 20190081120 | ISBN 9781459745186 (softcover) | ISBN 9781459745193 (PDF) | ISBN 9781459745209 (EPUB)
Classification: LCC PS8571.I476 S24 2019 | DDC jC813/.6—dc23

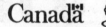
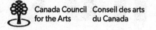

We acknowledge the support of the Canada Council for the Arts and the Ontario Arts Council for our publishing program. We also acknowledge the financial support of the Government of Ontario, through the Ontario Book Publishing Tax Credit and Ontario Creates, and the Government of Canada.

VISIT US AT

 dundurn.com |  @dundurnpress | dundurnpress | dundurnpress

Dundurn
3 Church Street, Suite 500
Toronto, Ontario, Canada
M5E 1M2

For Pam and Ed and Finn, who are together in the clouds.

CHAPTER 1

MOST PEOPLE THINK cumulonimbus are the best cloud-watching clouds, but Dad and I prefer cirrus spissatus. If you ask me, the whole cumulus family of clouds is too obvious. It's like they shout danger when anyone can tell they mean trouble at first glance.

But cirrus spissatus clouds are hypnotic. They promise mystery and hope: a thin veil between earth and heaven that might dissolve at any moment. We most often see Mom in the long, thin cover of the cirrus spissatus clouds. We seek her out every day, unless it's cloudless, of course, which means she's giving us the *all clear*. It's like a contest to see who can find her first. Maybe her face is our good luck charm or the act of looking is our prayer for the coming day.

When I was little Dad used to beat me to her, but now I find her first. When I do, when I point her out in some distant cloud formation, he sighs and, with a dreamy distant look in his eyes, says: "She's the most beautiful woman in the world."

And not until then, not until one of us sees her face in the clouds, do we start our day.

I lie back in the sun with my hands behind my head and scan the sky above me while Tuff dozes in a patch of dappled sunlight farther up the slope. The leaves overhead sift the sunlight across his body in a trembling pattern. His legs jerk slightly and I wonder if he's chasing a dream squirrel or a rabbit or maybe a raccoon. There're so many critters to chase and new places to explore in the ravine, I don't think he misses the boat at all. But I do. I miss the slap of the waves on the hull and rocking in a half-doze on the glinting sea. I miss Dad, too. But never mind.

I slip the last soda cracker into my mouth and chase it with a mouthful of water from the Tropicana jug. Then I empty crumbs from the plastic sleeve into the palm of my hand and eat those, too. I expect the rustling to wake up Tuff, but he's oblivious to me, whining in his sleep.

When I finish scouring the northern horizon, my eyes drift east. I split the sky into quadrants and search for her that way. North, east, west, and last of all, south. Dad prefers to let his eyes wander across the sky randomly, following her clues from thought to thought. But my way's faster.

"There she is, Tuff." I point out her face near the edge of the eastern horizon, beyond the overpass. "She's smiling today and her hair is streaming in the wind. She sure looks beautiful." I say it for Dad and then stand up.

Finally Tuff raises his head and assesses me from his patch of sunshine and green grass.

"Well, c'mon. Up you get. We can't lie around here all day. We've got stuff to do."

Tuff devours a bowl of kibble while I pack the tent and zip it closed. Then I pull the branches over the front door until it's completely hidden. It would take a psychic, or maybe a U.S. Marine, to find our campsite.

I pat my front pocket for my phone and charger. Then check for the lump in my back pocket, which is a small fold of twenty-dollar bills and the credit card.

"Everything's in order. Let's go!"

Tuff follows me out to the trail and up the side of the ravine, sniffing at every stalk of grass and tree trunk like he's met them all before and has to say hello to a long-lost friend.

"Don't get too used to living on land."

He tilts his head and barks once.

"Of course, I'll always take you for walks so you can chase squirrels."

As if to demonstrate his joy, Tuff races up the side of the ravine and stops at the base of a stately maple tree. He stares into the branches and dances around the trunk, trying to get a sightline on whatever he chased up there. When I get too far ahead, he abandons the tree and runs to catch up.

It's a glorious summer day. The sun is warm and bright without making the day oppressively hot. It's the air quality in Toronto that surprises me most. Even though it's July, the clarity of the air makes me feel optimistic and it's easy to breathe. It's never like that in the Keys, or even farther north in Tampa. No, the air in Florida is thick and heavy, and you can't ever forget that you need your lungs to survive. The summer air in Miami could sear your throat if you inhaled too deep.

When we get to the cemetery, I clip the leash onto Tuff's collar and head toward Bloor Street. I haven't been in Toronto long, but I already know the major intersections and basic landmarks downtown. I know the names of some of the neighbourhoods and can find my way to a few places.

There are even a couple of people I see day after day. Like the girl who sits on a square of cardboard near the intersection of Yonge and Bloor, her legs folded like a pretzel and her back as straight as the wall she melts into. She sits on the same block, though not always in the exact same place. Today she's on the northeast corner. As I turn onto Yonge Street, I look at her and nod. Tuff sniffs at her cup of change and I tug lightly on his leash.

"It's okay. He's cute," she says and reaches out to ruffle the fur behind his ears. I let Tuff introduce himself.

"Sorry. I don't have any change," I say apologetically.

"No worries. I'm happy meeting your dog. What's his name?"

"Tuff Stuff."

She wrinkles up her nose. "What sort of name is that?"

"My mom named him when he was a puppy because he was always trying to show the bigger dogs that he was boss."

"Is he?" She leans close and wraps her arms around Tuff's neck. He sits down, happy to be adored by a pretty girl. And she is pretty, despite the layers of dark clothing hiding her petite frame and the rings of black eyeliner that make her look like she's scowling. It's obvious she wants people to think she's badass, even though I can tell she isn't. Not even her black dreads or eyebrow rings can camouflage her perfect smile.

"Is he what? Tough?"

"Yeah, and the boss?"

"Not really. He's a pushover."

The girl unknots her legs and stands up. She reaches out her hand. "Lise Roberts," she says.

I hesitate and Lise chuckles.

"It's okay. I don't bite and I wash every day. *With soap.*"

A hot blush washes over my cheeks and I take her hand.

"Harbour Mandrayke. Nice to meet you."

"You should stop and talk sometime, when you have a few minutes," Lise suggests. "I think Tuff would like it."

Tuff leans against her leg with a hopeful expression and points his muzzle up at her like a wolf getting ready to howl at the moon.

"I will," I say and pull Tuff down the street after me.

＊　　　＊　　　＊

When I walk into the library I stop and take it in — the wide-open lobby, the stacked floors overlooking a cluster of study tables, the sunshine streaming down through the skylights. I love the way the staircases curve and rise like waves from one floor to the next, how the tidy stacks of books are moored in place like rows of boats in a marina. But more than anything I love that there are so many books waiting to be read.

Before I head to my favourite pod, I stop by the washroom. The washroom on the fifth floor is always empty and I feel more comfortable having a wash when nobody else is around. I don't imagine it's every day you find some girl having a bath out of the sink. But seriously, it's a pretty nice washroom for a public place. I plug the drain with a ball of paper towel and fill the sink with warm water. Then I lather up with soap from the dispenser and scrub my face before I take a wad of paper towel and, as Dad would say, wash my bits and pits. It makes me wonder where the girl on the street washes — Lise. I mean, she said she washes every day *with soap*. Does she have a favourite washroom on the top floor of some obscure building?

When I get to the pod, I plug in my phone to charge and pull up "Harbour's Summer Reading List." Dad compiled a list of books on ancient philosophy that will take me a couple of months to get through. I guess you could say I'm home-schooled, but not in a traditional way. I don't exactly excel at routines and neither does he. Like, we don't do a little bit of math and English and science every day. Some days we don't do anything at all but fish or snorkel or find a new place to moor. No, we tend to grab on to a topic until we're both ready to move to the next one. Before our ancient philosophy phase we spent four months in the forward cabin dismantling and assembling a 1977 Porsche 911 3.0-litre, air-cooled, flat-six engine. I mean, you never know when you're going to break down on the side of the road in your 1977 Porsche 911. Right?

The next book on the list is an autobiography that I've been looking forward to. Dad read me a few passages when I was a kid so I'm expecting it to feel something like a homecoming. Paramahansa Yogananda's auto-biography is a thick, sturdy book with a fair heft to it and will probably take me a couple of days to get through. Even though it was published in 1946, it feels like it was written yesterday.

I slouch in my chair and read about Yogananda's childhood. I'm completely mesmerized. It's like you can feel his wisdom and inner peace radiating from the pages. Almost two hours slip by before I start to feel hungry. When my phone is fully charged, I tuck it into my front pocket. Then I take a small knife out of my pocket.

"I'm sorry, Yogananda," I whisper before I cut the bar code and microchip from the spine, tuck the book into my day pack, and head outside into the warm summer day.

CHAPTER 2

THE SPORTING GOODS store has an insane number of sleeping bags. Who knew, right? It's kind of mind-boggling. After thirty minutes of reading labels and feeling overwhelmed, a bearded man asks me if I'd like any help. He's one of those super-outdoorsy types: tanned, wiry, intense. I'm a bit suspicious of his hair hygiene, which is significant coming from someone who's been washing out of a sink at the public library for three weeks. But his hair is so, well … long and messy. It's like he forgot he has hair to take care of at all. I wouldn't be surprised if something with four legs is living in it. He could be packing a pet hamster or ferret.

"I need a really warm sleeping bag," I tell him. "Like, suffocatingly warm."

The store is jam-packed with so much camping equipment and military gear there's hardly room to move. The sleeping bag display is crammed between the hiking boots and the hunting knives. There are about fifty sleeping bags hanging from the ceiling in what would best be described as a hallway.

"Where will you be sleeping and what time of year?" he asks as he stops beside me.

Despite his appearance and lack of attention to grooming, this guy makes me feel at ease. Maybe it's the bushy beard that feels familiar. Or maybe it's because he's dressed super casual in shorts and a T-shirt with brown sandals on his feet. He could have just stepped off a sail-boat in Key West.

"Let's say I wanted to sleep outside in the winter? Like, here, in Toronto?"

His eyes leave my face and scan my body. I can feel him assessing my clothing, calculating my height and weight. I'm surprised sleeping bags are so specific. I wonder if they're customized.

"Will you be in a tent or roughing it?"

"Roughing it?"

"Like, exposed to the elements?"

"Oh. No. I'll be in a boat."

"Is this hypothetical … are you really planning on sleeping in a boat in the winter in Toronto?"

"That's the plan. But I get the sense you think there's something wrong with it?"

"Nothing wrong, I guess. It's just that most Canadians store their boats in the winter, due to the lakes freezing over."

"Even the big lakes freeze over? Like Lake Ontario?"

The man nods and presses his lips together as if he's delivering catastrophic news. It makes his moustache and beard touch so that his mouth completely disappears in facial hair. I wonder if Dad knows about the ice issue in Canada during the winter. I make a mental note to talk to him about it next time he calls and wonder about starting a list on my phone. I already have quite a few things to talk to him about: did he remember to charge the auxiliary battery at the first of the month; does he still have a spare phone; ask him again why I had to come to Toronto alone (I'm seriously starting to wonder how he talked me into this); and now, did he know the lakes freeze completely over in Toronto, including the Great Lakes?

"I take it you're not from around here?" the man asks, interrupting my mental list-making.

"No. I'm from Florida."

He nods, as if everything suddenly makes sense, then turns to consider the sleeping bags hanging in front of us like discarded condoms.

"In that case, I would suggest one of our higher-end bags. Probably a hybrid. The synthetic keeps the moisture out and the down layer keeps you warm. Probably something rated to twenty below. I mean, it doesn't often get that cold, but that's what I'd get just to be safe." He turns the bag inside out as he speaks to show me the down-filled liner.

"You mean, like twenty degrees below zero? Celsius?"

He nods again and pulls at his beard thoughtfully. I shift my weight from one foot to the other and the wide, worn floorboards groan in response.

"Wow. That must be really cold. I mean, I remember one time it got down to like forty degrees Fahrenheit. We were up north, near Panama City. And I thought that was a cold night's sleep."

"If you think that's cold, then I definitely recommend one of our warmest bags."

"I need two. One for my father, too."

"How big is he?"

"Six feet. Hundred and eighty pounds."

The man pulls down one of the bags and starts to explain the hood and drawstrings. He shows me the inner pocket and tells me about how to decide whether to get a left-zip or a right-zip bag. He explains how the quilting is offset to eliminate cold spots.

"I had no idea sleeping bags were so scientific," I say when he pauses between facts.

"For cold weather they are. I mean, we have one that's good for forty below. It's for camping on the side of a mountain. There's nothing worse than being cold all night when you're out in the winter."

I feel the sleeping bag he's picked and wonder if it's really as warm as he says. If it's not, I suppose we can always come back and buy a second liner. And there's a space heater in the boat, so that will help.

"I'll take two. Both right zips. One for me and one for my father."

The man pulls two small nylon bundles from a cupboard. Stuffed into sacks they look remarkably small and I stare at them doubtfully.

"That's the great thing about down bags. They're lightweight and extremely compact," he says, as if he needs to rescue his sale.

When he rings them in, the total takes me by surprise, but I do my best not to react and hand over the credit card as if spending several hundred dollars is no big deal. I don't want him to start asking too many questions. While he deals with the credit card machine, I add another item to my list of things to talk to Dad about: don't flip out about the price of the sleeping bags.

The man examines the card and looks up at me.

"So you're H. Mandrayke?"

I smile and nod. "Harbour."

"Cool name," he says and finishes the transaction.

* * *

On my way into the library I drop Paramahansa Yogananda's autobiography in the returns bin. It lands with a thud and I look around to see if anyone has noticed. I feel awkward with an overstuffed day pack and a sleeping bag tucked under my arm. An elderly man at a nearby table looks up, but then goes back to his magazine just as quickly. Relieved, I climb the stairs to charge my phone and find the next book on my reading list. I haven't been sitting long before I notice a set of legs in my peripheral vision, but I don't look up from reading.

"Excuse me? Miss?" A librarian is standing beside me, holding Paramahansa Yogananda's autobiography in her hand.

I swallow hard and my heart gives two heavy thumps to make sure I feel suitably guilty about taking a knife to her book. I sit up straight and try to look, I dunno, *studious*. I don't want her to ban me from the library. Dad gets annoyed when I don't take my reading list seriously.

"I think you were the last one to read this book?" she says softly and gazes at me directly, but not with an accusation in her eyes.

I nod and glance down at the book in my lap.

"Did you enjoy it?"

Her question is so unexpected I look back at her face. She's leaning against the pod, which disarms me further. I lean toward her and speak in a low voice.

"I did. Very much. I found myself believing that Yogananda could actually move physical objects and influence events with his thoughts." I pause, then add dreamily, "or maybe I just wanted to believe in a world like that."

She considers my comment a moment then examines the book as if she's never seen it before. "We don't get a lot of people interested in this book."

"That's too bad. I think more people should read it. Maybe *you* should read it?"

The librarian glances down to where my next reading list book rests on my knees.

"Do you mind me asking what you're reading now?"

I blush. "His translation of *The Bhagavad Gita*."

She smiles and covers a laugh by clearing her throat.

"Are you taking a course on religion?"

"No, not really. My dad put it on a reading list for me. It's pretty good. You might like it, too."

"Your father sounds very interesting. I'm sure there are a lot worse things you could be reading."

She pauses and it gives me time to wonder what she means by "worse things." Is she implying that *The Bhagavad Gita* is somewhere on the continuum of bad to worse in terms of literature? But I don't have a chance to question her about what is on the far ends of her spectrum because she starts speaking again, and averting her eyes suddenly. She looks at her hands and then off in the distance, and finally at the floor to the right of my chair.

"Anyhow, I wanted to ask you to please stop cutting the bar codes off our books. If you want to borrow one, you could get a library card and take it home with you. I mean, it's a public library. That's what we do. We loan books to people. It doesn't cost anything. But we like to keep track of who has the books."

I want to tell her that I know how libraries work, but I'm also aware that, despite the fact that she's busting me for defacing public property, she's somehow on my side. She seems like one of those big-hearted librarians who believe the world would be a better place if everyone just read more.

"I'd love to get a library card."

Her expression brightens and now that she's finished delivering the bad news, she looks at my face again.

"On your way out, why don't you stop at the front desk and I'll help you with that."

I see my phone needs another half hour to charge fully.

"I'm not quite ready to go, but when I do …" I pause and note that her nametag identifies her as Erica. "… Erica, I promise to come and find you."

Dad is a big believer in using people's names when he talks to them, even complete strangers. He says if you use a person's first name it helps you remember that person better, and it also helps you get what you're asking for. I've seen him do it a thousand times and it always works. He oozes charm. His signature move is lowering his voice when he asks a person their name, then, if he's close enough, placing his hand on their forearm ever so lightly while repeating back their name like it's the most beautiful word he's ever pronounced. By the time he asks for whatever he needs, the person is nodding and smiling, bending over backwards to help him. If you can believe it, I've even seen him charm a coast guard that way.

Erica smiles and tugs her sweater down over her mid-section. She adjusts her glasses with one hand and nods to signal her departure.

"Thank you so much for helping me," I say as sweetly as I can.

She turns to leave but pauses. "One more thing, if you don't mind. Is that your dog tied up down the street under the tree? The border collie?"

I try to keep my cool, but suddenly I'm worried about Tuff. If something happened to him, well, I don't know what I'd do. I must look panicked because she puts her hand on my shoulder to calm me.

"He's fine. I just wondered if it would be okay if I took him a bowl of water? It's so hot today and I just thought if he had water other people would know he's being looked after."

Shame courses through my veins until I feel dizzy. I'm thankful to be sitting, otherwise I'm sure I'd have to find something to lean against for support.

"He's hasn't even been out there two hours. I would never abandon him."

"I know you wouldn't. It's just that I love dogs. So if you don't mind, I'll slip out on my break and give him a bowl of water, maybe introduce myself. Is he friendly?"

"Very. His name's Tuff. He likes girls, so watch out he doesn't fall in love with you."

Erica smiles shyly and slips away. I pick up my phone and start counting down the minutes until it's fully charged. *The Bhagavad Gita* is going to have to wait.

*   *   *

Erica is at the information desk by the front door when I'm ready to leave. When she sees me, she pulls a stool up to the computer and starts to type.

"Are you ready to get your library card?"

"I sure am," I say with what I hope is an abundance of enthusiasm.

She taps at the keyboard and nods at the sleeping bag under my arm.

"Are you going camping?"

"Yes. With my father."

"Where?"

The question takes me by surprise, but I've always been good at improvising. I try to picture the maps of Ontario we looked at when we planned this trip.

"Some park. Up north."

"Algonquin Park?"

"Yeah, that's the one. Have you been?"

"I'm not much of a camper. I like beds and showers too much. Now, the first thing I need is your name."

I tell her my name and spell it for her too, slowly. I like that Canadians know how to spell Harbour, even though almost everyone stumbles over Mandrayke. In Florida I had to explain every time that there was a *U* in Harbour because my mom was Canadian. Erica, though, doesn't flinch at either name.

"And your address?"

I scramble around in my head to come up with an address as quickly as possible. I'm acutely aware of the fact that a long delay will reveal me as a fraud.

"Nine Amelia Street."

I think about the house on Amelia Street that I've passed several times on my way to and from my camp in the ravine. It's just a cottage, really, but whenever we pass by Tuff insists on sniffing every inch of white picket fence, then peeing on the gatepost. It means I've had time to study this house: the stone walls, the yellow door, the high-peaked roof. I'm not really a house person, but this one makes me feel happy for some reason. It makes me wish, briefly, that we didn't live on a boat.

"Postal code?"

Now I pause for real. There isn't a chance I can come up with the postal code and I know it.

"Oh. Ummm. Darn. We just moved here and I haven't memorized it yet."

"Do you have any identification with your address on it?"

I shake my head and try to look disappointed.

Erica glances left, and then right. Finally she leans across the counter.

"I'm not supposed to do this, but I'll make an exception because I don't want you to get behind on your father's reading list. Next time you come in, bring something with your name and address on it. Just to prove you live there. Then I can finish off your card."

"So I can't sign out this book?" I make my face register more disappointment than I feel.

"I'll give you a temporary card today. Just don't forget to bring something like a piece of mail next time you come in."

*   *   *

Tuff and I are back at camp, lying together like spoons in a patch of filtered sun. I'm reading and he's dozing. I can feel his chest rise and fall with each breath and the fur on the top of his head tickles the soft underside of my chin. With each breath I inhale the familiar scent of his dogginess, a smell it seems I have known my whole life. We are lying on a layer of sun-warmed leaves and the feel of the earth beneath us is oddly comforting for a girl who's spent more time living aboard a boat than living on land. It's no coincidence, I think suddenly, that we call it the "ground" because lying on it makes me feel exactly that — grounded. Even though I'm still a stranger to the city, the ravine feels like home and at this very moment I feel uncharacteristically connected.

I'm reading a guilty-pleasure sort of book that sucks me into the story without intellectual protest. I sigh with the contentment of a perfect moment and lay the book on my chest. I still have Yogananda's *The Bhagavad Gita* to read, but for the moment I'm lost in this novel I borrowed from a book nook in Cabbagetown. You have to love a city that provides free books in tiny cupboards on random streets. I close my eyes and stare at the shades of orange and red inside my eyelids. It's been a busy day, but I feel satisfied that I accomplished so much. I purchased the sleeping bags like Dad wanted, I charged my phone, I signed out a library book — with my very own *almost official* library card — and I picked up some groceries. I won't have to leave camp for a couple of days.

My thoughts start to swirl. Images surface and then dissolve in my mind. I see the stone house on Amelia Street and wonder how I remembered that address when I was pressed by the librarian. I see Lise sitting on her square of cardboard, and the temporary library card Erica handed to me with a smile. I've never had a library card before, at least not since I was really young and we lived in that house on Pelican Way. I see my mother in the kitchen making me a grilled cheese sandwich for lunch. I can smell the dill pickles she cuts up for the side of my plate. I see my father steering the sailboat along the Intracoastal with the sun behind his back and smell the salty sea on the breeze. I'm riding the waves of a dozen overlapping images and scents and falling into a peaceful sleep when I feel Tuff stiffen and raise his head. A low growl rumbles in his throat.

I'm alert immediately, but don't move. I listen closely. The sound of distant traffic on the highway is always audible and normally I tune it out. But now I hear the car engines, like an endless single note, droning in the distance, punctuated with the impatient percussion of horns. I hear a lawnmower somewhere above and an airplane overhead in the distance. There are voices of children playing soccer at a park down the ravine and the wail of a siren beyond that. Then there are the sounds of snapping branches and crunching leaves. My heart starts to pound an ancient, panicky beat.

I scramble to my feet quietly, but crouch low and look in every direction. I know I'm vulnerable camped out in the ravine with just Tuff to protect me. I will my heart to slow down and peer under the thick undergrowth that hides my camp from the view above, but I can't see anything unusual. I rise slowly and scan the foliage, but I can't see the flash of colour that might give away a person approaching. Tuff leans forward and his ears signal concern. I gauge the distance to my tent, but am too afraid to move for fear of making a noise. Instead, I grab my phone and press in the digits 9, then 1, and leave my finger hovering over the 1. Tuff growls louder and is about to bark when a voice rings out.

"Hey! You guys wanna doughnut?"

CHAPTER 3

Lise pushes her way through the thick foliage and steps into the clearing where Tuff and I have made our home the past few weeks. She's wearing the same dark layers of clothing as usual and carrying a small flat box.

"Nice hideaway. Took me forever to find you."

She lifts the lid of the box and presents it to me.

"Do you like doughnuts? My friend works at a coffee shop and gives me the day-olds for free. They're still good."

She steps closer and I look down at two rows of variously decorated spheres of fried dough.

"That's a Boston Cream, my personal favourite. I highly recommend it."

She points to a chocolate-covered doughnut, but I don't move or speak. I'm still recovering from the intrusion. There hasn't been another human in my personal space for weeks. Tuff adjusts faster than I do. Once he realizes there's no danger, he wags his tail and edges close to Lise. He's such a traitor when girls and food are involved. I swear he used to be a player in a past life. And, like a teenage girl meeting a rock star, Lise responds to his advances. She balances the box in one hand and reaches down to rub his ears with the other.

"If you don't like Boston Cream, there're some jelly-filled, a cruller, a double-chocolate — *so good* — and an apple fritter. Go on, take one."

I glance at the selection, then back at Lise. As far as I can tell, she poses no threat and just the sight of the doughnuts makes my stomach rumble. I pick out a jelly-filled.

"Not sure what kind of filling you'll get but, if you ask me, there's no such thing as a bad jelly-filled."

I bite into the doughnut and icing sugar floats down over my shirt. I wipe my chin then quickly take a second bite. Lise waits to see my reaction.

"It's really good!" I say, through a mouthful of sweet, powdery dough.

"What flavour?"

"Lemon, I think."

Lise picks out the cruller and hands it to Tuff. Always a gentleman, Tuff takes it and lays it on the ground. He sniffs it and licks it, then flips it over with his nose for further inspection. He's not a picky eater, just cautious.

"Hilarious! I've never met a dog who didn't wolf down a doughnut in, like, two bites."

Lise picks out the Boston Cream, then closes the lid. She sits down cross-legged on the ground beside Tuff and, not sure what else to do, I sit down, too. I sneak glances at her, but otherwise we eat in silence. When she's finished, Lise wipes her face with her sleeve and looks around.

"Cool set-up. How long you been here?"

"Four weeks."

"You ever get scared down here by yourself?"

I balk at the truth. "I'm not by myself. Tuff's here."

"True, but still, you ever get scared?"

"I didn't until you came crashing onto the scene."

Lise nods at the obvious irony, hesitant to smile.

"If you ever do get scared, there's a shelter not too far away. It's pretty good. They don't ask many questions and as long as you're in by eight you're guaranteed a bed and a hot meal."

Lise offers me the box again and I take the double chocolate.

"Good choice," she says and takes the apple fritter for herself. Tuff looks hopeful, but she doesn't give in, even when he uses his saddest eyes.

"What kind of shelter?"

"A shelter for homeless youth."

It takes me a second to understand what Lise is saying, and more importantly, what she's implying.

"But I'm not homeless."

Lise glances over at the tent and presses the corners of her mouth into a scowl.

"I can see you're well equipped. But if you ever want a hot shower, maybe even a hot meal, there's a place you can go. That's all I'm saying."

"I'm okay. Really. This's just temporary. My home's on its way."

Lise stops chewing and narrows her eyes like she's trying to solve a riddle. She tucks a bite of doughnut in her cheek.

"Tell me how that works, exactly?"

"I live aboard with my father. He should be arriving in the next couple of weeks."

"You live aboard what?"

"A boat."

"What kind of boat?"

"A sailboat. A thirty-eight-foot Catalina."

"Where's he coming from?"

"Miami."

"Let me recap in case I'm missing something. You and your dad live on a big-ass sailboat and he's bringing it up from Miami *by water* and then you two are going to live up here?"

I nod and smile, a slight, embarrassed sort of smile. I'm used to this reaction. I haven't met a lot of kids who grew up living on a boat. There were lots, like down in the Keys, who spent family holidays on their boat. And I met a few who were aboard for a year or two, sailing around the Caribbean so their parents could take a break from the rat race. But by the time kids get to my age, most sailing parents settle on land so they can send their kids to a proper secondary school. For reasons Dad and I can never quite figure out, a lot of people are inexplicably obsessed with getting what might be considered a formal education.

"Either you're, like, totally delusional or you think I'm naive, to swallow such a ridiculous story." Lise shakes her head and licks her fingers clean.

"What's so crazy about living on a boat?"

"I didn't know people lived on boats. Not, like, full-time."

"Dad and I've been living aboard nine years."

"So why didn't you just sail up with him?"

I try to ignore the doubt flooding my veins and stand up.

"That's a long story. For another day," I say with more optimism than I feel.

When I wipe bits of leaves and grass from my clothes, Tuff jumps up and begins to dance. It's like he can smell a walk on the breeze. Lise looks at me from her spot on the ground, but she doesn't move.

"What?" she finally says when I put my hands on my hips and look impatient.

"Let's go down to the lake. I guarantee there're people living on their boats down there. Lots of land people have a kind of boat blindness. They notice a bunch of boats tied to docks and they think, *look at all the boats*. But they don't see the boats individually and they certainly don't see the people living aboard. It happens to us all the time. It's okay though, we like being invisible."

Lise doesn't budge but opens the box of doughnuts one more time. She considers her choices before she takes a jelly-filled and bites into the side of it. "It's a long walk down to the lake, you know?"

She offers me the box, but I pat my stomach. There's only so much dough I can swallow in one sitting, even if it's free.

"You've never been down to the lake, have you?"

Lise finishes her doughnut in two quick bites then jumps up like she's ready for a challenge.

"I been down to the lake plenty of times. After two years I been just about everywhere in this city. Good and bad."

She starts down the side of the hill at a fast pace and heads for the footpath that winds along the bottom of the ravine like a snake. Surprised, I scramble after her, and Tuff trots along at my heels.

$$* \qquad * \qquad *$$

The sidewalks and parks along the lakefront are crowded with people. There are people pushing strollers and long-boarding, people licking ice cream cones and taking photos, and people bunched up in chaotic groups clogging the way and making it hard for others to pass. Lise and I slip through the crowds unnoticed until we're standing at the very edge of the lake. Or rather, we're above the lake on a cement pier and the waves are slapping the wall below our feet. Even though the air lacks the saltiness of the ocean, just seeing boats bobbing on the waves and the sunlight glinting off the water makes me feel happy.

"Check it out. There *are* a lot of boats down here," Lise says.

It's true, the harbour is busy with traffic: sailboats and motorboats, a couple of Sea-Doos and even a passenger ferry. I sit down on the side of the pier and let my feet dangle over the side. Lise does the same and for a few moments we watch the boats criss-crossing in front of us. She pulls the box of doughnuts from her day pack and offers it to me first. I pick out another jelly-filled. There are two left. She takes one and hands one to Tuff, who accepts it gratefully.

"What's your boat look like?"

I study the boats in front of us and in the distance, then shake my head.

"It's not like any of these. C'mon. I bet we can find one farther along."

I get up and tug at Tuff's lead. Lise lifts herself to standing and follows. We cross over a metal bridge spanning a small basin of water. I lean against the railing and point to a sailboat a couple of docks away.

"It's that size but a different shape. Our cockpit is larger and we have a Bimini cover."

Lise laughs. "I have no idea what you just said, but it sounds like a sick boat."

"It's an older model, but Dad keeps it shipshape. We've redone the upholstery and Mom replaced two of the portholes with her stained glass."

A motorboat putters under the bridge and we watch it move below our feet and then out onto the lake.

"What's on the inside?"

"There're forward and aft cabins for sleeping. Mine's the forward one. There's a small galley as you come down the stairs. And a head off to the right."

"Hold up, Captain Harbour. Can you use regular-people terms?"

"Sorry. There's a little bedroom at the front of the boat. That's mine. Dad has the bedroom at the back under the cockpit — the place you steer from. When you first come down the ladder from the cockpit there's a little kitchen — *the galley* — and a washroom — *the head* — and then there's a sitting area just past the galley, with couches and a table."

Lise whistles her appreciation. "Sounds *fan-cee*. And this boat you're talking about, it's on its way to Toronto, right this very minute?"

"Yep. Right this very minute," I say, even though for the first time something feels wrong.

"Does your boat have a name on the back like these ones?"

"We call it *Starlight*."

"Pretty," Lise says. "Maybe I can have a ride when it arrives?"

"Sure. We can go for a sail and maybe moor over-night by the island or something?"

Lise and I walk farther along the lakefront, dodging tourists who are too busy looking around to notice us slipping between them like salmon going upstream. I've only known her a few hours but already it feels much longer. When we pass by a hot dog cart, Tuff raises his nose in the air and stops.

"I'm with Tuff. I could really go for some street meat," Lise says. "Too bad the guy I know works up at Yonge-Dundas Square."

We stand downwind from the hot-dog cart and my stomach votes with Lise and Tuff. It's been a while since I've eaten a thick, greasy hot dog. I think about the stash of bills tucked in the secret pocket of my jeans, but I leave them hidden. Dad said it was for emergencies and I doubt a hot dog craving would count. But Lise has another plan and starts rummaging in a nearby garbage can. She pulls out a coffee cup and wipes it clean with the tail of her shirt.

"Two hours tops and we're feasting on street meat."

She sits down on the edge of the sidewalk and crosses her legs. Then she digs a few coins from her pocket and places them in the cup in front of her. When she's settled, she pats the cement beside her. The invitation makes me feel nauseous, but I hide my shock. Or at least I think I do.

"Don't worry," she says when I don't move. "I got this. You go look around for a bit. But can you leave me Tuff?"

"Tuff?"

"Oh, sure. Tuff will make this go a lot faster."

I hand the leash to Lise and tell Tuff to stay. Then I walk away, looking back every few steps to see that Tuff is watching me but not protesting. I stand at a distance, but Lise motions for me to keep going. So I walk a little farther and sit down on a bench to watch.

I'm no expert on panhandling, but even I can see that Lise is good at it. She smiles and thanks people when they drop coins in her cup and sits as if she's invisible when people look away. Somehow she can become whatever people want to see.

It isn't long before three young children stop to meet Tuff. They approach cautiously, squeal "he's so cute" then kneel down and shower him with attention. They speak all at once.

"What's his name?"

"How old is he?"

"Where did you get him?"

The parents, trapped in an awkward situation, dig into their pockets. They look uneasy when they drop change into the cup and do it as quietly as possible so their children might not realize what's really happening. No parent wants to explain that the dog is homeless, never mind the girl.

When there's a gap in the foot traffic, Lise peers into the cup. The rest of the time she treats it like it isn't even there, like it's a stranger sitting on the sidewalk. Only once do we make eye contact and then she shoots me a thumbs-up so quickly I'm not even sure it really happened.

Two hours was an overestimation. Within an hour, Lise not only has enough cash to buy hot dogs, she has enough to buy us each a Polish sausage, and the vendor gives Tuff two free wieners that have been cooking too long to sell. Lise piles every type of condiment onto her bun: onions, olives, hot peppers, relish, mustard, ketchup, chopped tomato, and lettuce. It's clear that she's making as much of a meal of the condiments as the sausage. I dress mine a bit more conservatively and then we walk to a nearby park and sit under a tree to eat.

"Oh my god! This is the best sausage I've ever eaten," Lise mumbles. Mustard and relish drip down her wrist and she licks herself clean between bites.

Lise is right. The sausage is so good I can't force myself to slow down and talk. I eat straight through the sausage and bun and moan with pleasure. When I'm finished, I pull a bottle of water from my day pack and take a long drink. Then I hand it to Lise and she takes a swig, too. Finally, I pour a little into the coffee cup and offer it to Tuff. We laugh when he tilts his head sideways and laps at the water.

"I haven't felt this full in a long time," I say and stretch out on the ground. "All those doughnuts and then the sausage. That felt good."

"What have you been eating?"

"Soda crackers and canned tuna."

Lise fake gags but I know she wouldn't pass on any food that was offered. She can't afford to be picky and neither can I.

* * *

That night when we get back to camp, Lise talks me into doing something I haven't done since living in the ravine. She convinces me to build a small campfire. For the first half hour I jump at every sound in the dark underbrush, certain we'll be found, but soon the cheery warmth makes me glad I let Lise talk me into taking the chance. The glow from the flames flickers off her face, making her look more animated than she did during the day. She sits on the ground and breaks branches into small sticks that she feeds into the fire constantly, keeping the flames at a steady level.

"I can't remember the last time I sat around a campfire," I muse.

"I know a couple of guys who camp down at the Port Lands and they have fires every day. I never get to sit around at night, though. You know, 'cause I have to get to the shelter by eight."

I check my phone and Lise notices. It's already past her curfew.

"It's okay. I can sleep out tonight. It's no big deal in the summer. I have places to go."

"You can stay with me in the tent?" I suggest suddenly.

Lise looks surprised by my offer and, to be honest, I surprise myself, too.

"Sure. We'll be like a couple of Girl Guides," Lise says. But before I can reply she adds: "You sure you don't mind?"

"I'm sure. I have two sleeping bags and some crackers and tuna for morning."

"Dude! What's with you and fish?"

I can't help but laugh. I do eat a lot of crackers and canned tuna. For one thing, they last forever and travel well. Secondly, tuna and crackers keep me full longer than other convenience foods.

"Dad and I eat a lot of fish. It's the best source of omega-3 fatty acids. When the fishing's good we catch it and eat it right on the boat."

"Let me guess, you cook it in the *galley*?"

I laugh. Lise has a good memory.

"Sometimes we barbecue it. Sometimes we even eat it raw, fresh out of the ocean."

"Seriously?"

"It's sushi!"

"Canned tuna is one thing, but there's no way I'm eating raw fish. Not even if it's free."

We lapse into silence and watch the flames dance above a glowing bed of embers. Tuff is curled up at my feet, keeping them warm, and Lise lies down on her side, cupping her body around the fire. She props her head on one hand and has a faraway look in her eyes.

"Where did you live before Toronto?" I ask.

"Out east in New Brunswick."

"Why'd you leave?"

"Nothing to stay for."

"Family?"

"Not really. I was with my mom 'til I was about eight. Unfortunately for me, she wasn't really the mothering type." Lise laughs bitterly.

"Like, what did she do?"

"It wasn't so much what she did as what she didn't do. I pretty much fended for myself until a teacher caught on to me bringing Coke and potato chips for lunch every day. That's when the proverbial shit hit the fan. I bounced through a few foster homes after that."

"What's a few?"

"Twelve."

I don't know how to react to the idea of living with twelve different families so I say nothing and poke at the fire with a stick. Lise takes a deep breath and continues.

"Yep. It's exhausting. Moving every few months. Going to new schools. Learning new rules. Taking care of other people's kids. Having to pretend you're grateful. I just got so freaking tired of it all. When I turned sixteen I figured I could take better care of myself. I left my last foster home after a huge fight about how much toothpaste I was using and hitchhiked west with a guy I knew."

"Where's the guy?"

"That's a long story. For another day," she says, shrugging off the memory, but letting me know with a sideways grin that we are now even in the *hidden pasts* department.

Despite Lise's casual tone, the mood turns melancholy and I know better than to press for more information. The trick is to change the topic and the mood in one grand gesture.

"So, do you like music?"

Lise flashes a tough-girl scowl at me. "Everyone likes music."

I pull my phone from my pocket and scroll until I find what I'm looking for. Then I shift over and sit beside her.

"My dad's an insanely good musician. Watch this."

I press play and Dad's face appears. He's scrunched as small as he can make himself so he fits the screen and he's holding a ukulele near his face, strumming and humming. I took the video on the boat one night when we were goofing around. I actually have a small collection of E.D. Mandrayke's ukulele serenades. After a few bars of music, he breaks into a jazzy version of "Somewhere Over the Rainbow." He's smiling from ear to ear and singing right at the camera so that I feel like he's with me for real. My heart aches whenever I see his face and hear his voice, but I can't help myself. I shift my gaze from the phone to Lise and I see her smiling in response. It would be impossible not to. Dad has that effect on people, especially when he sings. It's his own brand of charisma. Lise hasn't smiled like this all day. I mean, I've seen flashes of smile but not sustained like this. I put my phone away when the song ends.

"That's your dad?"

"That's him."

"Weird. I sort of thought you made him up. You know? The whole boat story and all? But that's really him, huh?"

"It really is."

"And he's really coming up here in your sailboat."

"He really is."

"He seems great."

"Wait 'til you meet him in person."

CHAPTER 4

THE NEXT TIME I leave the ravine, it's to run more errands. But first I fill Tuff's water dish so I can give my face and hands a good scrub. I never really considered it when we lived on the boat, but it's hard to keep clean when you live in a tent on the side of the ravine without so much as a mud puddle to splash in.

I lean over the dish and scrub my face twice, hoping I've erased all signs of camp life.

"Hey, Tuff," I say when he comes to see what I'm doing with his dish. "Remind me to find a mirror."

When I've done what I can with my face, I examine my hands. I've bitten my fingernails so short there's no white crescent and my cuticles are red and ragged. Dirt is caked into every crevice and crack, and it takes the rest of the drinking water to get them clean enough to go into a store.

"Let's go, Tuff," I say, whistling for him when I'm finally ready.

Although I need to replenish my water supply, the main purpose of my trip is to get more dog food. There's only enough kibble for two or three more meals so if I don't buy some soon, I'll have to start feeding Tuff from my supply of crackers and tuna. And although Tuff will eat just about anything, he's not a big fan of fish.

I head for Food Basics, a discount grocery store I discovered my first week in Toronto. It has the lowest prices and isn't far from the ravine. It's also close to a gas station where I can fill up my water jug.

As a general rule I try to avoid grocery stores because there're too many temptations. Even when I walk the aisles knowing I can't afford anything but dog kibble, I crave all sorts of foods I haven't thought about in weeks: ice cream, yoghurt, cheese, grapes, fresh bread. I do my best to resist, but in the end I pick up a jar of generic-brand peanut butter and a small bunch of bananas. The peanut butter will keep in the tent and the bananas won't make it back down to the ravine.

The cashier rings through the items and I hand her the credit card. I stare at the headlines on the magazines while I wait, headlines that are meant to sucker people into buying whatever crap is written inside. But who really cares which celebrity has the most cellulite and which one cheated on his wife? Like Dad, I'm convinced the IQ of the average person is plummeting.

"I'm sorry, but your card has been declined," the cashier says.

My heart flash-freezes.

I stare at the card in her hand, but I don't take it from her. "Can you try again, please?"

The cashier, who is not much older than me, tries again. I appreciate that she doesn't roll her eyes or sigh impatiently, so I wait politely. It's hard to look calm when your insides are twisting like a tornado. This time while I wait, I don't read the magazine headlines. I focus on the credit card reader. Time has shifted suddenly and the seconds tick by at an agonizing pace.

After what feels like an hour, she pulls the credit card back out of the machine and looks sympathetic. "I'm really sorry. It says it's declined again."

I look at the three items on the conveyor belt and try to process this information. Even though I'm craving peanut butter and bananas so badly my stomach is turning inside out, I know I can live without them. If I'm careful, I have enough crackers and canned tuna to get me through a couple more weeks. But Tuff needs to eat.

"I'll just take the dog food," I say and rummage in my pocket for the emergency twenty.

The girl puts the peanut butter and bananas on the counter beside her and hands me the change: three dollars and twenty-five cents.

"Sorry 'bout that," she says. When she sees me steal a longing glance at the bananas, I know she really does feel bad.

Tuff waits patiently under the tree where I tied him up until he sees me come out of the grocery store, then he starts to dance and whine. I was only out of his sight for fifteen minutes, but I feel just as relieved to see him. I lean down and bury my face in his fur. Tears burn like fire in my eyes, but I take a deep breath. Just the smell of him keeps my heart from racing even in the wildest of storms.

There are only two things that really matter to me in the world. I've got Tuff in my arms, but where's Dad? Cold fear has been scratching at the bottom of my stomach for days and no matter what I tell myself, I can't make it go away.

Tuff tucks his tail between his legs when I reach over to untie the leash. He always knows when I'm upset and this makes me feel worse. I need him to stay upbeat. For a split second all I can think about is running down the street and disappearing into the ravine, tumbling down the steep slope and hiding among the tangle of thick vines. I want to hide away and worry in private. But for the moment I can't make myself walk. It takes every ounce of control to keep breathing and to keep the tears from spilling down my cheeks. Instead of escaping, I sit down at the base of the tree with the dog food on one side and Tuff on the other. I have no idea what's happening, but I know something has gone wrong. Dad's missed two Sunday calls, he's weeks past his arrival date and now the credit card has been declined. Tuff lies down beside me and rests his chin on my leg with a quizzical whine. I rub his ears absently while I try to think. But it's hard to concentrate on anything beyond the trembling that has taken over my limbs.

Suddenly Tuff lifts his head. I look up to see a man standing beside us. He's a young man — older than me — but I can tell by the way he's leaning against the tree trunk that he's not exactly doing the adult thing yet, either.

"You okay?" he says with so much concern a lump jumps up the back of my throat.

I nod and swallow, trying to clear a path for the words to come out.

"You don't look all that okay," he says, then kneels down. He has a gentle way about him and it isn't long before Tuff stretches his nose forward until he's almost touching the man's fingertips. Tuff sniffs his hand and takes a step forward.

"Are you a good boy? Are you?" The man croons until Tuff is wagging his tail so hard his body looks like it's going to turn inside out. Then, like a total traitor, Tuff rolls onto his back for a belly scratch.

"I have a dog at home who looks just like this," the man says, glancing at me and smiling. He has smooth light-brown skin, soft brown eyes, and a smile that transforms his face into boyish mischief.

I try to smile back but it's hard with tears threatening to overflow my eyelids. Instead I dab at my eyes with my fist and I tug Tuff back to my side. The man eases himself casually to a stand, opens his wallet and offers me a twenty-dollar bill. I want to protest, explain that I'm not panhandling, that I just happen to be sitting on the sidewalk. But the words are elusive and despite the shame burning in my cheeks, my body betrays my intentions. I watch in horror as my hand reaches up to accept the money.

"Thanks," I whisper, while looking down at a piece of gum flattened on the sidewalk beside me.

The man doesn't move away, but digs a scrap of paper from a nearby garbage can and writes on a crumpled green flyer for *Best Piano Lessons with Wing Chong*.

"I don't know what sort of trouble you're in, but you look like a nice girl and I hate to see you upset. If you ever need help, just call me. Or text. My name's Brandon. I *always* answer. Day or night. And I live close by."

He hands me the paper and I glance down to see he's written his name and a phone number, and drawn a cartoon dog with a big smile and its tongue hanging out.

"So, what's your name?" He tilts his chin upwards as he asks me this.

"Hillary," I say instinctively and offer a soggy smile, hoping to hide my lie.

"Well, Hillary. It's been nice to meet you and your dog. I hope we meet again."

He walks away a few steps before stopping and looking back. "Don't lose that number," he says and winks. Then he mimics holding his phone: "Text me."

I flutter the flyer in front of my face. "I've got it."

Tuff watches him go, but I stare back at the flyer in my hand.

✳   ✳   ✳

When Lise finds me I'm lying in front of the tent staring up at the sky, refusing to think about how I caved, how I went back into the grocery store with that twenty to ease my cravings. I've eaten a quarter jar of peanut butter, as well as all four bananas, so at least I'm not hungry. She sits, then leans back and stretches out in the sun. I like when she comes down in the afternoons before her theatre district shift. It's nice to have the company and she always brings something to share. One time she brought a big bottle of Coke and another time she had a bag of oranges. They had brown spots and were a bit withered, but they were still juicy and sweet inside.

"How was your day?" she asks.

Tuff comes to greet her and wriggles between the two of us. He licks Lise's face. She giggles and tries to push him away.

"Not great. How about yours?"

"Excellent, actually. Look what someone gave me."

She pulls a twenty out of her pocket. I swallow my shame and brighten my expression.

"Seriously? Someone gave you that?"

"Yep. It was some old lady. She said she sees me all the time sitting on the street and it makes her worry about her granddaughter who's my age and lives in Vancouver. And that's not all. She gave me a sandwich and a chocolate milk, too."

She reaches into another pocket and hands me a foil-covered packet. "I saved you half the sandwich, but I drank the milk."

I sit up and take the sandwich. It's homemade with thick slices of bread and triple layers of ham and cheese.

"I can't remember the last time I ate cheese."

"I know, right? I almost went out after and bought a whole block of it."

When I'm finished, I hand the last bite to Tuff. I can never refuse those brown eyes. Lise chuckles when he takes the bite of sandwich away to inspect. Suddenly her eyes widen.

"Is that peanut butter?"

I hand her the jar. "Help yourself."

She twists open the lid and scoops out a finger full.

"There're crackers in the tent," I remind her.

"It's better this way," she says and pops the glob in her mouth. "God, I love peanut butter. Where'd you get it?"

"At a grocery store. I had to buy some dog food and I couldn't resist."

I think about the four bananas and vow to be a better friend. I mean, if she can save half a sandwich for me, the least I can do is save her a banana.

She looks at me with a question in her eyes. I've never explained how I acquire things and she's never asked, but I feel a sudden need to tell her about my day.

"The awful thing, though, is that my credit card got declined."

I want to tell her about the twenty dollars, too, but for some reason I can't bring myself to admit that I bummed money from a stranger, even if it was by accident.

"Wait! You have a credit card?"

"I *had* a credit card, until this afternoon. For essentials. Like dog food and minutes for my phone. Dad wanted to make sure I could get what I needed until he got here. But it got declined today. I used my last cash to buy the dog food."

"Your *last* cash?" Her back stiffens and her eyebrows dip.

"I'm sorry I didn't tell you before. I just …"

"I know. You wanted to make sure I wasn't going to murder you in your sleep and take off with your canned tuna." She laughs and I feel even guiltier thinking about the small stash of bills in my secret pocket. I only have a hundred dollars left, but I have no idea how long it has to last. Still, a hundred dollars would feel like winning the lottery to some people.

"I promise I'll make it up to you when Dad gets here."

"I know you will," she says and lies back down in the sun. She lets Tuff lick the last of the peanut butter off her finger and stares at the clouds floating overhead.

"So where does your dad get the money to pay for the credit card? I mean, it doesn't sound like he has a regular job and someone has to pay the bill?"

"My grandfather owned some radio stations in the southern states. Florida and Georgia mostly. Dad inherited them before I was born. They make enough for us to live on."

Lise glances over at me and starts to laugh. It's a deep uncontrollable laugh that bubbles up from the pit of her stomach. I replay the conversation in my mind to figure out what's so funny but the expression on my face makes her laugh even harder. After a couple of minutes she's holding her stomach and trying to catch her breath.

"Are you messing with me?"

I shake my head. "They're just small. Except for WEDM in Miami. But most of that went to my step-uncles."

Lise becomes still all of a sudden. "You're telling the truth, aren't you? Just when I think you can't get any stranger, you up and tell me your family owns a bunch of radio stations. What else you got to hit me with?"

"My great-great-grandfather was the governor of Georgia. Like, back in the 1930s? Before that my father's family was just a bunch of Georgia crackers."

"Georgia crackers?"

"It means they've been in the south forever. I'm descended from one of the families who first settled Georgia.

Mostly they were farmers. Grew corn, herded cattle. That sort of thing."

"And your mom's family?"

"I don't know much about them. She died when I was little."

"The most notable person in my family was an uncle who owned a corner store in Fredericton. Until some big chain came along and put him out of business. Then he ended up on welfare like everyone else."

We fall into silence and watch the clouds thicken and build overhead. It feels like hours go by before one of us shifts our position. Every now and then Lise chuckles and shakes her head like she's about to ask me another question, but then falls silent before it can slip out of her mouth.

"Why do you think the card got declined?" she asks finally.

"I've been thinking about that. Maybe dad lost his phone so he can't pay the bill."

"That would explain why he hasn't called in a while."

Dad's terrible with phones, it's true. He won't even try texting and I can't count the times I've seen him lose one over the side of the boat. I mean, it happens a few times a year. He either leans over to tie off a rope and it falls out of his front pocket, or he fumbles it when he's dialling and it ends up overboard. The part I don't tell Lise, though, is that he'd have no way to replace it if he did lose it. Dad never goes ashore. I haven't seen him on land for over four years. I'm the one who runs his errands, but now he doesn't even have me.

"Do you ever look for things in the clouds?" Lise asks unexpectedly and brings me back to the moment.

"Every day," I say and feel the cold scratching in my stomach again.

"Look! See that clump over there?" Lise points to the far right where a band of cirrus spissatus has merged with an approaching mound of cumulonimbus.

I look over and nod. I haven't been able to see much in the clouds lately. In fact, I haven't seen Mom's face for three days. But I know it's my mood getting in the way, not that she isn't there to find.

"Don't you think it looks like your dad with his ukulele?"

*　　　*　　　*

The ravine at night is a different creature than during the day. I like how darkness scrabbles down from the neighbourhoods and spreads across the valley floor, seeping into every crevice and nook like ghost crabs hiding in the shadows. What I don't like up top is how the street lights mask the darkness, cloaking people in a sense of purpose while they scurry and scuttle from place to place.

To me the ravine is more real than the streets; it's gritty and primal. Every night I hear creatures scratching in the undergrowth around our tent. At first these noises bothered Tuff and frightened me, but now we know there's nothing to fear. The rustling leaves and chirruping raccoons are just part of the backdrop of noise, along with the car engines and sirens.

I feel lonely lying alone in the dark and wonder about texting Brandon, just to say hi. He was friendly, approachable, and having a conversation with an actual person, even by text, would take my mind off things, for a few minutes, anyway. I dig the coloured flyer from my pocket and start to write a text, but then I delete it and flick to my music files instead.

What I really need to cheer myself up is a dose of Dad. Tuff perks up when he hears Dad's voice singing "You Are My Sunshine" and I try to show him the screen, but all he wants to do is lick it. By the time the song finishes, the jitters I felt earlier in the day disappear and I chastise myself. How could I doubt him? Dad is a survivor. I know he's closing in on Toronto, motoring on the still days and sailing when the wind co-operates. Any day my phone will ring and I'll hear his voice telling me to pack up camp and get my butt moving. I can't wait to see him. I can't wait to introduce him to Lise and move back into my forward cabin. It might be small, but it's mine and I feel safe tucked up under the bow of *Starlight*.

I'm still lying in the tent with the front flap open and flicking through pictures of Dad when a scream splits the night. I drop my phone and sit up. Not far away I hear a girl swearing and the sound of a struggle unfolding in the fallen leaves. Tuff growls and I grab a leather bundle tucked at the bottom of my backpack. All I can think is that Lise is in danger and bolt from the tent after Tuff.

It's easy to find my way to the commotion, even in the dark. As my eyes adjust, I see a broad, hulking figure dragging something off the trail into the bushes, but that something is writhing and twisting in protest. Tuff rushes forward, growling and snarling. I had no idea Tuff could sound so fierce, but the rage in his throat raises the hairs at the back of my neck. He snaps at the hulking figure and the man's anger turns. He kicks and swears while Tuff darts in and around his feet. He has his arms wrapped tightly around Lise's face and body, so as he twists and turns she gets flung about like a rag doll. Above the sounds of Tuff's attack and the man's defence, I also hear Lise whimpering. I'm not sure if the man is aware of me watching but I know I have to do something and I have to do it fast. I pull out my Glock 17 and shout as loud as I can: "Let her go *now*, you scumbag, or I'll shoot your balls off."

Startled, the man stops moving. He stands completely still and for a minute all I can hear is Tuff snarling in the darkness.

Then he sneers. "What you gonna shoot me with, *bitch*?"

Dad always tells me not to let my temper rule any situation. He also tells me not to let stupid people make me do something I'll regret later and that name-calling is a symptom of weakness. But all his good advice is forgotten when I hear the word *bitch*. Of all the names I can tolerate, *bitch* makes my pulse spike. That's why I do the only thing I can to fight back. I raise my gun and fire.

The shot shatters the night and just about shatters my eardrums, too. Tuff yelps and the man drops Lise. He sounds like an elephant crashing through the undergrowth and I know he's not going to look back.

The next thing I hear in the darkness is Lise's outrage.

"What the *hell* was that?"

I rush toward her, but she kicks away, deeper into the brittle undergrowth.

"It's okay. It's me, Harbour."

I try to find her in the dark but she crawls away on all fours.

"You just shot an effing gun at me!" she shouts. "You could have killed me."

Her breathing is ragged and the adrenalin is making her lash out whenever I get close.

"I shot in the air. It wasn't anywhere near you."

I stop moving for a minute. Trying to get close is making her retreat faster. Finally I approach again, slowly. She's panting and half crying when I finally get close enough to put my arm around her.

"C'mon. Let's go back to the tent."

She lets me help her up and I guide her down the slope in the dark. We stumble together over fallen trees and wipe leafy branches from our faces when they reach out to grab us.

"Are you okay?" I ask as we trip up over a hump of dirt, possibly a rotted stump.

"Of course," she says in her tough-girl voice. "But I almost shit my pants when you shot that thing."

I track the rim of the ravine and the lights of the cars flickering on the highway below in order to get my bearings, then I steer us farther right. With all of the commotion I didn't pay attention to where I was heading. When I feel Tuff back at our heels I'm relieved because if I get us lost, he can always find his way home.

"Shhhh." Lise stops and listens.

"What's the matter?"

I want to tell her not to worry because I doubt that perv will be back to mess with us anytime soon. But she shushes me again and stands dead still. She leans her face close to my ear.

"The cops are gonna be down here any minute. We should put some distance behind us fast." Her breath feels hot on my neck.

When we finally stumble across the trail that winds like a scar along the bottom of the ravine, we turn south toward the lake. She half pulls me behind her, but she doesn't need to worry about me keeping up because I'm in no mood to talk to the cops. After twenty minutes of running, we find a bench and sit down to catch our breath. If anyone questions us, we can say we're taking the dog for a walk. It's a reasonable story.

"Where the hell did you get a gun?"

"Dad gave it to me."

"What father in his right mind gives their kid a gun?"

"He wanted me to be safe. He taught me how to shoot when I was little."

"You can't just carry a gun around."

"Why not? It's our constitutional right. You know, the second amendment? The right to bear arms?"

"*Dude*, the second amendment doesn't cover Canada. Handguns are illegal here. You can get in serious trouble being a homeless kid with a gun. You're lucky they didn't catch you bringing it across the border."

I think about the border crossing and a slight shiver scrabbles up my spine. Thank God for Tuff. But I don't say this to Lise. In fact, I don't know what to say. I hadn't really thought about gun laws in Canada and I wonder if I need to take a trip back to the library to brush up on the basics. I'm sure Erica would be happy to point me in the direction of a good law book. I imagine her standing at the front counter, still waiting for me to arrive with a piece of mail so I can prove my place of residence. I also don't know how to respond to Lise because I don't think of myself as homeless. Instead of speaking, though, I rub my hands together and stare at a streetlight in the distance. It shines a cone of orange light onto the trail. Lise slumps over her knees in the thickening silence.

"Thanks for that," she says eventually. "Even if you did just about give me a heart attack."

*   *   *

When we're sure the coast is clear, Lise and I navigate our way back to camp. I left the tent in such a rush, I didn't get a chance to set up the camouflage or even zip the flap. So I'm relieved when nothing has been disturbed. By the time we crawl into our sleeping bags, it's past midnight and I've barely rolled onto my side before I'm pulled into a dream.

My dream is part fiction and part memory. It's a familiar dream and one I dread. I'm sleeping in my princess-pink bed in our house on Pelican Way. I'm little and everything towers above me. The desk hulks in the corner and the lamp arcs high above me like a giraffe. My stuffies are piled in the corner, but in the darkness the mound looks alive so I'm afraid. I've always been afraid of the dark and I want to creep across the hall into Mom and Dad's bed, but I can't move. I'm sure someone is in the room with me and I try not to breathe so whoever is there will be disappointed by the emptiness and go away. Then there's an explosion. It's so loud I cover my ears and

slide deep under the covers. There's yelling and screaming and I hear Mom pleading with someone in the next
room, though I can't make out the words. On the other
side of the wall things crash and glass shatters. A gunshot
rings out and I can tell by the muffled moans that someone has been hurt. I listen hard and pray that Mom and
Dad are safe, but I don't get to say "amen" because my
bedroom door flies open and my father lifts me out of
the bed. He wraps a sheet around me and hisses in a voice
that scares me into absolute silence.

"Keep your eyes closed. Don't move. Don't make a
sound."

Then he covers my head and carries me out of the
house.

I don't move or unwrap myself for hours. When I
can't keep still any longer, after I've wet myself and thirst
drives me to test the limits of my bravery, I peek through
an opening in the folds of the sheet. I see that I'm on
Starlight. But I already knew that because I listened to
waves smashing against the hull for hours before I finally
fell asleep.

I'm in the aft cabin alone, but light seeps from behind
the curtains so I know it's morning. I untangle myself
and stand to peek out the porthole. There's nothing but
ocean and sunlight stretching as far as I can see. I climb
off the bed and sneak over to the door. I turn the handle
slowly, quietly, and look into the main cabin where Dad
is sprawled, fast asleep on one of the benches. He is on
his side facing the hull and his shirt is caked with dried
blood. Before I know what's happening, I'm screaming.

"Harbour! Wake up! You're having a bad dream."

Lise is shaking me and when I open my eyes all I can see is darkness. Tuff is whining and straining to get close to me. It's a relief to realize I'm in the ravine again, although my pulse is racing and my shirt is soaked with sweat.

CHAPTER 5

WHEN I CRAWL out of the tent the next morning, Lise and Tuff are sitting by a campfire. Lise is breaking branches and Tuff is chewing a stick at her side. They both look up when I stumble into the sunshine, but Tuff doesn't stop chewing.

"What are you doing?" I ask. I don't mean to sound alarmed, but I obviously don't mask my anxiety well.

"It's just a little fire and I won't let it burn long." Lise uses my mother's eat-your-broccoli tone of voice, the one she used when she wanted to cajole me into eating something I didn't like: *Just try one bite. If you don't like it you don't have to finish.*

Lise continues to feed the fire, so I try again to get my point across.

"I just thought after last night, you know, we didn't need to draw more attention to ourselves."

Lise ruffles Tuff behind the ears and speaks to him directly as if I'm invisible.

"She's a worrywart, don't you think?" She stands up and sorts through a pile of sticks until she finds one she likes, then she breaks it in half.

"It's just that I'm pretty sure it's illegal to camp down here," I say, not trying to hide how annoyed I feel.

Lise sighs and rolls her eyes. "Relax! If anyone comes down and complains we just apologize and move on. I've been kicked out of lots of places before. It's no big deal. Anyway, come and sit down. I have something for you."

I want to tell her that I don't want to move to a new camp. I can't move. I want to tell her that my site was selected carefully, with Dad's input. But I know this won't make sense to her. It barely makes sense to me anymore. Instead of trying to explain, I sit reluctantly. That's when I notice a large coffee can in the middle of the fire, and, inside it, boiling water.

"Hot chocolate?" I ask.

"Better."

"Coffee?"

"Better."

Lise uses a stick to tip over the can of water and lift it from the fire. The embers sizzle and smoke spirals into the air. She sets the blackened can on the ground at my feet and, when it tips over, six eggs tumble out. Lise moves in on the eggs and picks one up, using the sleeve of her shirt for protection.

"Let's eat them while they're still hot."

I pick up one of the eggs and juggle it from hand to hand until it is cool enough to peel.

"Where'd these come from?"

Lise eats her first egg in two quick bites. I'm surprised to discover they're soft-boiled, which is my favourite kind of egg *ever*. If only I had some toast to dunk in the yolks.

"I was bringing them down last night when that guy jumped me. I went and found them this morning. Only a couple were broken, but Tuff took care of them."

Lise peels her second egg and Tuff watches us hopefully, his head resting on his paws and his eyes flickering between me and her.

"You bought them?"

Lise nods and bites into her second egg.

"We've got a busy day ahead of us. You're going to need the energy."

"What busy day?"

"Think of it as an outing."

"What kind of outing?"

"You'll see."

*　　　*　　　*

After breakfast Lise takes me and Tuff to a rundown area near the waterfront. At some point it had obviously been industrial because there are boarded-up factories and sprawling warehouses forgotten behind vine-covered fences. There are signs of revival, though. We pass a treed area where the grass has recently been mowed. There are picnic tables and benches and a paved bike path winding through. There's also an old brick warehouse under renovation with glimpses of everyday life visible through the wide expanse of windows: white blinds, an oversized abstract painting, and minimalist light fixtures hanging from long wires. We skirt around a parking lot where there are half-a-dozen cars, and a coffee shop that has been created out of a narrow brick building. It has an outside patio lined with flowerpots and colourful umbrellas.

Lise ducks behind a rundown cinder-block structure and squeezes through a hole cut in a tall mesh fence. The edges of the fencing have been peeled back, making it easier to go through one way than the other. We follow a trail through an overgrown lot.

I ask several times where we're going, but all she says is, "Wait and see."

Besides a web of footpaths, there are other signs of life around us. In a small clearing there's a metal drum that looks like it serves as a fireplace, and cement blocks circling like chairs. There's a pair of beat-up running shoes propped against a stack of bricks and a blanket draped over a pile of bald, cracked tires. Tuff trots ahead and sniffs around the fire barrel in a way that makes me think it's used for cooking.

"Franklin? Josh? You guys around?" Lise calls out.

A man pokes his head out of a boarded-up building and looks cautiously around until he sees Lise, then his face breaks into a smile.

"Lise Roberts! What's up, girl?"

He ducks to get through a hole in a sheet of weathered plywood that's been nailed in place to keep people out. When he straightens up and walks toward us, I see how tall he is, and thin. He moves as if his limbs were loosely connected by elastic bands and a leg or arm might fall off at any moment. He and Lise exchange some sort of secret handshake before Lise turns to me.

"Frankie, I'd like you to meet my friend Harbour. Harbour, this is my man, Frankie."

Frankie needs a shave and looks like he could use a good night's sleep, too, or maybe a week's worth. It's hard to tell how old he is. He could be Lise's age or he could be Dad's age. He looks weathered like Dad but acts twenty years younger. He's wearing jeans and a baggy green T-shirt that proclaims EVERY DAY IS EARTH DAY. He wipes his hand on his jeans, then leans over to shake mine. Even his fingers are skeletal.

"Harbour, eh? Nice meeting you."

Tuff, who has been sniffing around the periphery of the lot, returns when he hears an unfamiliar voice.

"This is Tuff Stuff," Lise says.

Frankie leans down to introduce himself and Tuff is a perfect gentleman. He sits quietly and soaks up the attention so thoroughly that Frankie looks reluctant to stop rubbing his ears.

"Awesome dog. I love his eyes."

Tuff does have great eyes. When you look into them it feels like looking into a human soul. Maybe it's because they look like they are rimmed with black eyeliner. Or maybe it's the pattern of black that frames his tan face, but Tuff always has a question in his eyes. Right now I'm sure he's asking, *Who's the tall dude and is he safe to be around?*

"Where's Josh?"

Frankie jerks his head in the direction of downtown. From the overgrown lot we can see the tops of the tallest skyscrapers that line Bay Street, and beyond, the spike of the CN Tower.

"He went to collect some cash and cocktails. You wanna hang around? We trapped a rabbit for dinner."

Up until this point I haven't said much but now I can't help myself.

"Like a wild rabbit?"

"A wild *city* rabbit, but it tastes just the same as any other rabbit."

The thought of eating some poor wild creature, like the kind I've been sharing the ravine with the past few weeks, turns my stomach. Lise must sense my reluctance because she interrupts Frankie's explanation about how Josh trapped the rabbit.

"There won't be enough meat for all of us on one rabbit. But I got enough cash for a pack of hot dogs. What do you think, Harbour? Feel like a wiener roast tonight?"

I nod, even though I'm not sure I want to hang around with two strangers all the way until dinner. I mean, it's probably just past noon. But what can I say when Frankie is watching me with so much hopeful expectation?

"Okay, it's settled. Harbour and I will go get some wieners. We won't be long. You can start working on the fire."

Lise and I follow a trail west, in the direction of downtown. We wind deeper into the industrial area, through shaggy, overgrown fields, past looming piles of dirt covered in tarps and tires, across empty parking lots where weeds push through aging tarmac, and even over a set of railroad tracks that don't appear to be in use any longer. She seems to know where she's going, so I don't ask any questions. But while Tuff trots at my side on a slack leash, I try my best to track the top of the CN Tower. I always like to know where I am and how to leave, just in case.

"So how do you know Frankie and Josh?"

"Frankie was at the shelter when I first arrived. He knew Josh already."

"Are they from here?"

"Frankie, I think, is from Windsor and Josh from somewhere up north."

The trail ends at an empty rubble-strewn lot and we have to scoot through an opening in a chain-link fence before we step onto a sidewalk where, despite the fact that I feel as though I've emerged from a post-apocalyptic world, people appear to be going about their regular lives. Across the street there's a grocery store. It looks out of place next to a cluster of cement silos, but who I am to judge what belongs where?

"When's the last time you actually roasted hot dogs over an open fire?" Lise asks as we head for the entrance.

"Maybe never?"

"I guess fires don't really mix with boat life, huh?"

"We had a little barbecue off the cockpit that we cooked hot dogs on sometimes," I suggest, remembering grilling fish more than wieners.

I tie Tuff to a post near the entrance and we walk into the cool, bright store. Other shoppers glance our way, then look away too quickly. I know what this means and I control an impulse to flee. Lise leads us to the cold meats and grabs a pack of Red Hots.

"These ones are always the cheapest," she says, then grabs a second pack. I open my mouth to protest but she just shrugs. "Still only five bucks for both."

I grab two Snickers bars at the checkout — the extra-big ones. When Lise looks like she is about to protest, I shrug and say, "These are on me."

"Are you sure?"

I nod.

"But what about your credit card and food for Tuff?"

"I think I'll be okay." I toss one of the bars at her as we leave the store. "Besides, I'm starving."

The walk back to Frankie and Josh's feels faster than it did going to the grocery store. Maybe it's because I already know where we're headed or maybe because for the first ten minutes I'm occupied eating the chocolate bar.

"So good," I mutter as I swallow the last bite.

"*So* good," Lise agrees and licks her fingers.

Frankie has a small fire going by the time we return and Josh is back from his cocktail run, sitting on an upturned cinder block, watching the rabbit carcass. It's skewered on a metal rod and suspended across the opening of the metal barrel. He nods when we're introduced, but doesn't look at my face. Josh is Frankie's opposite. He's short and solid and he moves with efficiency. He watches the rabbit hungrily and I wonder if it will cook through before he starts tearing off the limbs.

We spend the afternoon sitting around the barrel talking under a low, grey sky and watching the rabbit turn from dark red to brown. Apparently Frankie likes having someone new to talk to because he tells me about how they've been living in the office of the boarded-up garage for almost a year.

"Never once went to a shelter last winter. Not once. Not even when there were extreme cold weather alerts." Frankie says this proudly, like they survived Dieppe, or maybe the Holocaust.

"One night it was so cold we sat up all night and kept the fire going," Frankie says. "I wanted to sleep, but Josh wouldn't let me. He was afraid if we did, we'd never wake up."

Finally Josh weighs in, as if he's suddenly decided the conversation is worth joining. "It happened to an uncle of mine once, you know. He was on his three-day trap run and the fire went out in the middle of the night. For some reason he never woke up. My father found him the next week in his cabin, frozen through, solid as cement."

"At least he didn't suffer, eh?" Frankie says kindly.

"Yep, at least he didn't suffer. Not like my grandfather when he got lung cancer. That was some nasty shit. I'd rather freeze."

Frankie and Josh pass a bottle back and forth all afternoon and into the evening. Twice it lands in Josh's lap empty and he disappears into the boarded-up building, returning with a full bottle. The second time he returns and tosses it across the fire Frankie fumbles and drops it on the ground.

"You got shit coordination," Josh mumbles.

Frankie takes a series of short nervous sips before defending himself. "It's hard to see in the dark."

"It's not that dark," Josh says, looking suddenly up at the sky.

I also look up at the sky and see it is, in fact, getting late. Darkness has fallen around the overgrown field and boarded-up building. The lights from downtown glow on the horizon.

Frankie passes the bottle back to Josh, who throws back his head and takes a long drink. It's a clear bottle filled with blue liquid, and when he's finished, he offers it to me.

"No, thanks," I say. I try to sound polite, but it's only been ten minutes since I last explained I don't drink.

Josh stares me down. "You American or something? Your voice sounds funny."

"Uh, yeah. She grew up in Florida," Lise interjects quickly. I can tell she's wary of Josh.

"My mother was Canadian, though," I add, which kills Josh's interest in my nationality.

Lise and Frankie both relax and Josh gets up to fetch more wood. He paces around the fire and turns the rabbit every few minutes. The flames lick up at it hungrily. Every so often a drop of grease hits the fire and sizzles, which makes Tuff raise his head and sniff the air. I can tell he's got plans of his own for that rabbit.

"You girls don't have to wait for us. Go ahead and break out your hot dogs if you want," Frankie says.

I look to Lise. I'm dying for a hot dog. It's been ages since I ate the Snickers and my stomach has been pestering me steadily for two hours already. I'm hungry enough to think the rabbit looks appetizing, even though it looks like a prop from some bad sci-fi movie with bared yellow teeth and hollow eye sockets.

Lise passes around the pack of wieners and we skewer them onto sticks. I hand one to Tuff and he goes through his regular routine of sniffing and inspecting it before he decides it's safe to eat.

"Lise says you have a camp in the ravine? Up by the cemetery," Frankie says when the conversation stalls. "She says you're gonna spend the winter on a boat with your dad?"

"That's right." I nod, suddenly uneasy that anyone knows about my camp besides Lise.

"Gonna get pretty cold. You know that, right? Like you maybe got another six weeks before your drinking water starts freezing at night. Best thing is to sleep with it to keep it thawed out. Travis taught me that."

Frankie looks around as if he's expecting to see Travis and I squint into the darkness, also half expecting someone else to show up.

"Are you expecting Travis and Charlene?" Lise asks.

"No way!" Josh shouts. "That asshat is *not* welcome."

Frankie and Lise share a knowing look that I can't decipher and Frankie quickly changes the subject.

"So you were saying your dad's coming up before winter?" Frankie asks.

"He'll be here long before then. I'm expecting him any day," I say with more confidence than I feel.

"You might want to have a plan B, just in case."

"I'll be okay. Dad's on his way."

When Lise and Franklin exchange a quick glance, a shiver scuttles down my back.

"I mean about living on your boat. The water lines will freeze and you'll get stuck for a couple of months."

"I'll let him know," I say.

Frankie takes a long drink of the blue liquid before he eats the hot dog Lise offers him. Having a full mouth doesn't keep him from talking. "I'm just saying, we spent a winter out here and it ain't no picnic, even for us, and we got a totally sweet set-up. Come have a look." Frankie unfolds himself from the cinder block he's been sitting on and gestures for me to follow.

He wobbles when he takes a step and Josh laughs. "Steady as she goes, bro."

Lise catches my eye and nods to let me know it's okay, and since I'm curious about what's inside, I follow

Frankie through the hole in the plywood into a dimly lit room that smells like damp earth and dirty socks.

Frankie flicks on a flashlight and sweeps it across a narrow space that's set up like a dorm room. There are platforms built from stacked blocks and scrap lumber, and on top of that are layers of cardboard and blankets. Beside each makeshift bunk are plastic crates covered in melted wax and items of clothing hanging on nails.

Frankie takes a box of matches from a shelf on the wall and lights a candle. The room comes to life in the soft yellow glow and he turns off the flashlight.

"What do you think? Pretty sweet, huh?"

He jumps up onto one of the bunks and I sit on a plastic lawn chair at the end of the other bunk.

"You guys set this up?" I ask, looking around.

He nods and stretches out. "Actually Travis and Josh set it up. Then Travis and Charlene started seeing each other and Travis moved out. So I moved in." Franklin pauses. "But I've made some improvements. Like these platforms. Josh and Travis just slept on the ground."

"Travis and Charlene are friends of yours?"

"Yeah, sorta. We used to hang around. But Josh is still mad about him leaving. So now they hang out with Mike more in High Park. It's too long a walk."

"So it gets pretty cold in the winter? Even in here?"

"Freeze your balls off." He pauses and considers me. "Well, really effing cold, anyway. But last year we rigged a wood stove with the fire barrel. Even made a chimney to vent the smoke."

He points to a round hole in the wall above my head that's blocked with pink Styrofoam.

"Stove works pretty good for this little space, especially when we cover the floor with cardboard for insulation. There's some pretty rough nights, for sure. But at least it's not a shelter."

"You don't like shelters?"

The candle flickers and my shadow lengthens and dances on the wall. Frankie shifts positions and lies on his side, facing me, his head propped on his bony hand.

"The men's shelter is nasty. Full of drunks and bums. The whole place stinks to hell and there's bed bugs. Plus you have to sleep in shifts to make sure nobody steals your stuff."

"Lise says the place where she goes is pretty good."

"The youth shelter. Yep, it's a pretty sweet deal if you can stick to the rules. But they boot you out at twenty-four. Expect you to get a life by then."

"I didn't know they had age limits."

"They got everything limits. When you can come in at night, when you have to leave in the morning, what you do during the day. No drinking or drugs, that's for sure. But you'd be okay. You don't drink."

"Is there, like, a lower age limit?"

"Sixteen. Before that they stick you in care. Talk about a nightmare."

"You were in care?"

"Everyone out here was in care at some point. Either that or they, like, lost the parent lottery or have some mental issue or something." He stops to consider his summary, then adds: "And some people just have plain old bad luck."

"You?"

"Definitely bad luck. I lived with my parents until they were killed in a car accident."

"I'm sorry," I say and study his face.

He winces, then falls into a deep dark sinkhole in his mind. "They were stoned," he says finally.

"How old were you?"

He wipes the hair out of his face. "Ten. I lived with my aunt after that. But then she met a guy and I got too tall and too ugly. I didn't fit into their plans for a perfect family."

"You're not ugly."

Frankie laughs and dismisses my attempt to humour him. "You need an eye exam."

"What about Josh?"

"You don't want to know his story."

"Why not?"

"His parents didn't get a very good start in life. They passed that on to him."

Frankie scratches his shoulder then lies back down and looks up at the ceiling. I follow his gaze, but there's not much to see besides water-stained plaster covered in smoke stains and cobwebs.

Lise's head appears through the hole.

"Hey, Harbour, we should probably head soon."

The tone of her voice sounds urgent so I get up and go outside. Frankie follows at my heels. The fire is blazing and flames are leaping out of the barrel. Josh is piling more wood on top.

"What the hell you doin', asshole?" Frankie yells and runs over to grab the pieces of lumber from Josh's hands. "Someone's gonna call the fire department if you're not careful. And where'd the rabbit go? Did it fall in the fire?"

Josh slurs something incomprehensible and begins scrabbling on the ground for the rabbit.

Frankie flails his arms and screams. "Jesus, you do this every time! Now what we gonna eat?"

In his quest to find dinner, Josh gets too close to the fire. His hair flares up and then dies down as he stumbles away slapping his head. He trips over the pile of lumber and falls in the long grass. Somehow, in the time we were inside, Josh had transformed from a low-key urban trapper dude into a raging drunk.

While Frankie works to beat down the fire with a two-by-four and Josh struggles to stand up, Lise leans over and hisses at me.

"Let's bounce. Now."

She heads across the lot without saying goodbye and I don't hesitate. Neither does Tuff. We scramble through the hole in the fence just as I hear Frankie say: "You idiot. You scared the girls away. You always do that. How many times I gotta tell you about making the fire too big? You wreck everything. I don't even know why I stick around. No wonder Travis left. "

Josh slurs a response and then it sounds like a fight breaks out. There are grunts and indecipherable shouts, and the sound of fists making contact with flesh. I slow down and Lise stops to see why I'm not keeping up.

"It sounds like they're going to kill each other. Should we go back?"

"We should definitely *not* go back. They won't kill each other. I promise. They won't even remember fighting tomorrow."

Tuff is lying at my feet chewing on something but in the dim light it's hard to tell what he has.

"Drop it, Tuff. Drop it!"

He drops the object reluctantly and I use the light from my phone to see the burnt rabbit carcass lying on the road. I kick at it with the toe of my shoe.

"How did he end up with this?"

"I dunno," Lise says. I can tell she's trying not to laugh. "But I say good for Tuff. Someone might as well enjoy it even though it looks disgusting."

"I kind of feel bad for those guys. I mean, this was supposed to be their dinner."

"Don't lose any sleep. I bet they got a stash of canned goods for emergencies."

We make our way through the deserted Port Lands toward the busy city streets, loud and crowded with young people headed out for a night in the bars. A car passes with a guy hanging out the back window. His hands are raised in the air and his chest is bare. There are arms reaching from inside, trying to drag him back through the opening while he shouts out at the street. "Screw you, assholes! This world is mine!"

I tuck my head deep into my sweater and try to blend in with the storefronts. But Lise flips the guy the bird and mutters, "Talk about assholes."

A few steps farther a cluster of girls in skin-tight skirts teeter out of a restaurant on high heels. They move over a little too far on the sidewalk when they see us walking past. If Dad were around he'd throw a compliment their way, but I'm too embarrassed to look at their faces and assume their giggles are about us. Lise senses my embarrassment and tilts her chin up in response.

"We got just as much right to be here as they do."

I nod and wish we were already in the ravine, in the darkness and safety of the tent. But we have ten more minutes before we even hit the trail. Eventually the crowds thin and we turn onto a side street. I sigh gratefully at the emptiness and feel lighter the farther away we get from the bright lights and bustle of a Saturday night.

"Do you hang out with them much?" I ask suddenly, my mind turning over the events of the day.

"Not really. I mean, they're nice enough until about ten, then they end up fighting, like, ninety percent of the time."

"What were they drinking?"

"Hand sanitizer and Gatorade."

"Hand sanitizer? Why?"

"It gets them drunk, faster and cheaper."

"Isn't it dangerous?"

"Yep. That's why they mix it with the Gatorade. To cut the alcohol content."

It takes me a few minutes to process this information, so we walk in step but also in silence. Finally Lise clears her throat.

"Don't go getting all judgy about it. There're worse habits. The rest of the time they're pretty good guys."

"I wasn't being judgy," I say defensively.

"Whatevs. The thing is, you can't afford to be picky out here. Those guys might be drunks, but they wouldn't hurt you. I'd rather hang out with a messed-up drunk than a violent one."

CHAPTER 6

LISE AND I are tidying up the campsite when she drops a bomb. "So how late *is* your dad?"

She's breaking branches into short sticks and I'm kneeling in the tent, taking stock of my supplies. The hairs on the back of my neck prickle and I freeze mid-movement the same way a hunted animal does when it wants to hide against the backdrop of the forest. She also stops moving and since we're separated only by a thin layer of nylon, I can hear her breathing and waiting for me to respond.

"He's not on an exact schedule. Sailing doesn't work that way."

I put down the can I'm holding and sit on the back of my legs, hoping whatever point she is driving towards, she will stop when she senses my reluctance to engage in a conversation about my father.

But she doesn't.

"Then how long since you last spoke?"

"I'm not keeping track," I lie and focus instead on the twenty-nine cans of tuna stacked neatly in the corner. I pick up a box of crackers to add to the pile of supplies. "But that doesn't mean anything other than he lost his damn phone again."

Lise resumes breaking branches and I hear the cracking and splintering as she busts them across her knee.

"Okay, but I've been thinking. If he gets way off schedule, like if he doesn't get here before the nasty weather hits, you're gonna need to consider coming to the shelter. And it would be better if you made a plan now for what you're going to do with Tuff if it comes to that."

My heart goes into overdrive and it's difficult to breathe. Even if I knew what to say, I feel physically unable to utter a sound. Lise crawls into the tent behind me and puts a hand on my shoulder.

"Don't panic. We're just talking. We just need to come up with a plan. Nothing is going to happen right away. You've got time to get used to the idea."

"I can't leave Tuff," I finally manage to gasp, then suck back a massive lungful of air to make up for holding my breath.

"I know you feel that way but there might come a day when you have to leave him for a night. Like what if you got hurt, or sick or something?"

"That's not going to happen."

"You're right. Probably nothing's going to happen. But I still think you should have a plan. So I was thinking maybe you could leave him with Frankie and Josh. Like in an emergency?"

I turn and glare at Lise like she's lost her mind.

"No way. They're not capable of taking care of themselves, not to mention a dog."

"Do you know anyone else?" Impatience starts to slip through the cracks of her calm facade.

I sit silent for a moment while I run through the list of people I know in Toronto. So far the list goes Lise, Frankie, Josh, Erica, and Brandon. Although I can't really say I know Erica or Brandon as much as they were both kind to me during a moment of crisis.

"Well?" Her tone is almost taunting and it makes me want to prove her wrong.

"I know Erica. She works at the library and she loves dogs. She might take him overnight."

"There you go, then," Lise says. "Let's go ask her."

Lise backs out of the tent on all fours and stands up so that I can't see her face. Then she waits, without even trying to pretend she's not waiting.

"What? Like right now?" I resist the urge to pick up a can of tuna and hurl it at her shins.

"Sure. No time like the present, right?"

I'm pissed at Lise for bullying me into doing something I don't want to do, but I have too much pride to admit she's right about my lack of resources. So I crawl out of the tent, zipping it closed behind me, and drag the evergreen branches over the sides as camouflage.

We head in silence up the trail that leads out of the ravine. Tuff must sense the tension between us because he keeps returning to our feet, looking from Lise to me, then barking. It's like he's scolding us for acting like a couple of children, or like Frankie and Josh. When we finally step onto the streets of Cabbagetown, some of the anger has drained out of me and I turn to Lise.

"Are you coming to the library with me?"

She nods and says sheepishly, "I'll wait with Tuff outside."

*   *   *

I'm nervous about seeing Erica because I know she's going to think I came to get my permanent library card and expect me to produce a piece of mail displaying my home address, complete with postal code, which I won't be able to do. And after the morning of tension, I'm not in the mood for lying. Still, I don't have much choice — Lise has me backed into a corner. So I walk into the library trying to look confident, and end up feeling smaller than usual in the gaping lobby.

I take a deep breath and cling to the small hope that Erica isn't working, but she is. When I glance over at the information counter she's the first person I see and her sixth sense must have had a recent tune-up because she looks up at the same moment I spot her.

Her face breaks into a smile and she watches expectantly while I drag myself toward her. My legs feel heavy, like my veins have been filled with hot lead and I'm wearing cement blocks instead of running shoes.

"Harbour!" She greets me brightly. "Did you bring in a piece of mail?" She doesn't say it, but implies the word *finally*. Or maybe I'm just imagining a hint of impatience.

I glance at the floor and pick at my cuticles. "No. I'm sorry. We rerouted our mail from Florida, but nothing's come yet. I promise I won't forget, though." I add weight to the word *promise* and muster as much false optimism as possible.

Erica leans forward and peers over the counter.

"Not checking out any books today?"

I shift my feet uncomfortably. "No, still on Yogananda's *The Bhagavad Gita*. It's taking me longer than I expected."

"I'm not surprised," she says. "That's a complex book." She taps at a computer keyboard lightly with her fingers. "So what can I do for you?"

"Actually, it's about my dog," I say reluctantly and look away again, this time behind the counter at a trolley of books waiting to be shelved.

When I glance back at her, her brow is furrowed with long deep lines. "Is he okay?"

"Oh, yeah. He's great. But I have a bit of a favour to ask. I mean, I hate to impose, but I don't know anyone else in Toronto yet and you said you liked dogs. So I just thought maybe you wouldn't mind watching him for a night? My dad and I have to go out of town and we can't take him. It's just this once. I'll bring food and his dish and everything."

Erica's shoulders fall. Her eyebrows pinch together, and she presses her lips into a grim line. It's obvious she has disappointing news she doesn't want to deliver.

"I'd help you out if I could. He's such a lovely dog. But I live in a very small apartment and the landlord has a strict 'no pets' policy. I can't take the chance. I'm sorry."

I can tell she really is sorry and I feel ashamed for lying to her, especially when she was so generous about letting me have the temporary library card in the first place. She's been nothing but kind to me and how have I repaid her? By cutting bar codes out of her books and lying to her face every time we speak. I force myself to smile as radiantly as I can.

"That's okay. We'll figure something out. I'm sorry I even asked."

By now there are three people behind me and Erica is definitely looking uncomfortable. She glances past me to the next person in line.

"I'll be back with that piece of mail soon," I promise.

When I step away from the counter, I'm angry at myself for lying, for failing, and for being stuck in a situation I can't control that makes me lie and fail. I want to go back and tell her the truth about everything, including that I don't really live at 9 Amelia Street. But instead I make my way through the front entrance and find Lise sitting off to the side of the doors with Tuff, a coffee cup on the pavement in front of her. I slouch down beside her.

"She lives in an apartment," I mutter. "No pets allowed."

Lise softens and rubs Tuff behind his left ear.

"Hey, it hasn't been a total waste of time." She picks up the coffee cup and dumps the change into her hand. "Two dollars and seventy-five cents. Not bad, for what? Like, fifteen minutes?"

Tuff wiggles over and noses my hand until I rub his head. The clang of change landing in the cup makes me stand up in a hurry. The last thing I want is for Erica to think I'm bumming change in front of her library.

"C'mon, let's go."

Lise stands up reluctantly. I know she'd be happy to spend a couple of hours sitting on the pavement, but I can't get away fast enough. I lead us around the corner to the back of the building.

"So who's this guy, Brandon?" she asks, trotting a few steps to catch up.

"I met him the day I got the peanut butter."

"How?"

"I was on the sidewalk with Tuff, upset about my credit card. And he stopped to talk to me."

I also remember the twenty-dollar bill he gave me, but I can't force myself to tell Lise the whole story.

"Do you know where he lives?"

"I have his number. He said to call anytime. Or text."

I pull out my phone and show Lise the number, as if to prove to myself, as much as to her, that I'm not a complete liar, and also to prove I don't need her as much as I actually do. We stop and lean against the wall of the library. Lise holds on to Tuff's leash and watches people walk by as I type: *Hey Brandon. It's me, Harbour. From the other day out front of Food Basics.*

I hit send and feel a nervous ball of heat churn in my stomach.

"Let's take Tuff to that park," I say, pointing across the street. "He can have a pee while I wait to see if Brandon answers."

The park is small. There's a bench, a patch of shaded grass, and just enough shrubbery to keep Tuff's nose entertained. We walk him around the edges of the garden beds and he stops in front of a cluster of tall green plants with pink blooms that are being investigated by two monarch butterflies. I breathe in deeply and recall with a sharp pang of nostalgia the fragrance of jasmine on the inky night air, a smell that reminds me of being home.

My phone vibrates and I take it out of my pocket: *Hillary?*

My face flushes hot. Another fib and one I forgot about telling. There's no way he'll want to help me when he realizes I'm an ungrateful liar.

"What's wrong?" Lise asks, reading my expression.

"I didn't give him my real name when I met him."

"You're smarter than I thought you were," Lise says. Her approval takes away some of the sting.

I stare at the phone, trying to figure out what to text when it vibrates again. Lise reads over my shoulder.

LOL. Whatever name you go by, how r u? Was hoping to hear from you.

"Tell him you have a favour to ask," Lise coaches.

"Shouldn't I text a bit more first? To be friendly?"

"Nah, just bite the bullet."

I type: *I'm okay but have a bit of a problem. Wondered if maybe you could help?*

Brandon's text arrives so fast I wonder how he even had time to type it. *Anything. What's up?*

I need someone to watch my dog for a night. I have something I have to go do.

Sounds mysterious. But sure. I can dog sit. Where are you?

A little park on Church St. Near Yonge. Do you know it?

Sure do. Be there in 15. Hang tight.

The exchange takes only a few minutes. We continue around the perimeter of the park and then sit on the bench. Tuff lies down on the grass and dozes.

"So who's this guy again?"

"Just someone I met. He started talking to me on the street. Tuff seemed to like him."

"But you only met him once for a few minutes?"

I nod.

"Why do you trust him with Tuff if you didn't trust him with your real name?"

I shrug. I don't know how to answer this. Maybe because he helped me out once already when he didn't have to. He was sweet and seemed genuinely concerned when I was upset. And he was well-dressed, even cute. But there's no way I'm telling any of this to Lise.

"Probably because he wasn't homeless," she says spitefully.

I bristle at the suggestion. "It's not that. But Frankie and Josh aren't very reliable. You can't argue with me there."

"Whatevs," Lise says, turning slightly away from me.

We sit for ten minutes without speaking before a black car pulls up in front of the park. A heavy beat of music comes from inside, but stops when the engine cuts off. Brandon steps out and lifts the sunglasses from his face.

"Harbour!" He calls out, then opens up his arms as if we're long-lost friends.

I stand up and walk toward him with Tuff while Lise stays on the bench.

"You're even more gorgeous than I remember," he says, then wraps me in a big hug. I'm surprised by his warmth, but I can't lie, it feels good to be held tight and he smells really clean. He pushes me away and drinks me in with his eyes. "So what sort of jam you got yourself into?"

"Not a jam, really. Just need someone to watch Tuff for a night. I've got to leave town and I can't take him on the bus."

He squats down and rubs Tuff's ears, talks to him like they're best bros.

"Tuff, my man. How's things? You want to come to Chez Brandon for a sleepover? We can watch some Netflix and get takeout sushi? I got a pretty sweet condo with a million-dollar view." Brandon laughs at himself and glances up to see my reaction. I smile broadly, but a beat too late.

Brandon turns back to Tuff. "She looks a little freaked out. Have you been taking good care of her …" He pauses and looks past me to where Lise is still perched on the bench looking pissed, then adds: "… and her friend?"

I turn and motion for Lise to come over and meet Brandon, which she does. But she saunters over slowly like she has all day to make the distance. I'm confused by her reaction. I know she trusts Frankie, but I didn't expect her to totally ice Brandon.

"Brandon, this is Lise."

Brandon stands up and gives Lise a quick up-and-down assessment. Then he holds out his hand to shake.

"Any friend of Harbour's …" he says.

Lise offers him a limp hand and mutters, "Nice to meet you," almost under her breath.

"So when you need this dog-sittin' favour?" Brandon asks, trying to sound all gangster, but failing to pull it off.

"Next week," Lise pipes up. "We've got a funeral in London. We just found out our grandmother died."

I hold my expression still and avoid looking at Lise so I don't accidentally contradict her peculiar story.

A look of disappointment washes over Brandon's face, then confusion. He studies Lise carefully, narrows his eyes, then turns back to me. "You two are cousins?"

"My dad was adopted," Lise offers. "Her dad was the real kid."

Brandon falls silent while he recovers from the sudden change in direction.

"Well, I'm sorry about your granny." His tone has changed slightly and I'm confused about what's going on, why I'm on the fringe of yet another conversation.

"She was pretty old," I offer. "Lung cancer."

"Still, I loved my granny. It was tough to say goodbye."

Brandon takes a couple of slow steps toward his car, then turns back. "My schedule's free all next week and Tuff's always welcome. You two want to come and check my place out? To make sure it's suitable?" He opens the door of his car like an invitation.

Again, Lise is quick to answer. "We have a few calls to make. A couple of cousins in Montreal to get hold of still. Maybe we can come over in a couple of days when we have our bus tickets and everything."

I'm so angry at Lise for dissing Brandon that I want to apologize before he leaves. But something in the set of Lise's mouth keeps me quiet.

"I'll text you the details when I know more," I say politely. "I sure appreciate you helping out like this."

"No probs," Brandon says. "You got my number."

With that, he climbs into his car and starts the engine. The heavy bass music pumps again and vibrates into the pavement. I can feel my insides pulsing to the beat. When he pulls away I turn to Lise.

"What the hell? Why were you being so rude?"

Lise turns to me and narrows her eyes.

"That guy's trouble. I can't believe you didn't figure it out before. It's a wonder you've survived this long without your dad."

My pulse sputters, then picks up speed.

"Are you that pissed because I don't want to leave Tuff with Frankie?"

"Absolutely not. But you let Brandon do one favour for you and I guarantee you'll be paying him back for the rest of your life."

"Are you jealous?" I stare hard at her, shocked that she could be so openly bitter about some random guy I met one time.

"I swear, you're more naive than I thought. Harbour, that guy just wants to use you."

"Use me how? By taking care of my dog? By letting me come and check out his place?"

"God, Harbour. Open your eyes. He's trying to charm you. He's being sweet and generous just to manipulate you into thinking he's a good guy. Then when you're in some sort of trouble he'll swoop in and rescue you so he can prey on your gratitude. There're guys like that all over the place."

"I think you're exaggerating. He's just trying to be helpful. That's all. He cares about people."

"Trust me on this one. Okay? I came to Toronto with a guy just like Brandon. So I know a bit of what I'm talking about."

Lise reaches over, rips the phone out of my hand, and presses a few buttons.

"What are you doing?" I ask, trying to grab it back.

She pushes my hands away. "Deleting his number. So you can't be tempted to text him."

When she's done, she hands back my phone and I stare at it in my hand as if it's betrayed me.

CHAPTER 7

WHENEVER THE DOOR to the theatre opens I catch a waft of warmth on my face and drink in the smell of indoors. It's a smell that reminds me of hotels and shopping malls, a smell that takes me back to when Mom was alive and we took family trips to Walt Disney World and SeaWorld, and one time to Universal Studios. It reminds me of being clean and safe and sure-footed. I used to feel like I could do anything. I used to feel like my confidence was about to spill over into the world. But now I feel it slipping away, draining a little bit at a time the way a bathtub empties when you pull the plug. How much longer until I'm sucked down the drain?

Smiling people and golden light spill through the glass doors. Shoes clack hastily on the pavement in front of us. The hems of suit pants and dresses swish past as if they don't have time for our puny problems. I pull Tuff across my lap and bury my face in his fur. He helps keep me warm and hidden. Lise pulls the blanket up over her shoulders and then reaches across to make sure my back is covered. It feels like I've been cold forever, and I'm afraid because, according to Lise, a chilly fall evening like this does not begin to compare to a cold winter's day. Moment by moment I feel more unprepared for what lies ahead. What was Dad thinking when he decided we would winter in Canada? Nobody heads north in the winter. Even the geese have started gathering and taking practice flights over the ravine, honking above the highway in search of a more hospitable climate. If I had wings, I'd hurry to catch up.

"It won't be long till the rush, and then we can call it a night," Lise promises.

I nod and wince when I hear the sound of coins hitting the bottom of the coffee cup in front of us. I'll never get used to the sound of shame.

"I'd guess we're at twenty-eight dollars so far. Not bad for a couple of hours."

Lise has an uncanny ability to tally the take in her head by the sound of the coins landing. She's impressively accurate. I haven't seen her make an error in two weeks.

"Thank you, sir," she says in response to another clatter of coins. Then to me she mutters under her breath, "Three dollars. Nice."

Lise cups Tuff's face in her hands and whispers in her baby voice. "This partnership thing really pays off. It must be this cute as *eff* dog." He whines in appreciation and thumps his tail on the pavement.

"What do you wanna do with this haul? I think we should celebrate."

She's talking to me, but because she's still holding Tuff's head and using her exaggerated tone it feels like she's asking him.

"I dunno."

But Lise persists in trying to spark my imagination — and my hunger. I know she's trying to keep me from slipping further into the shadows of the alley behind us.

"Fruit and bread?" she suggests, trying to lure me into her game of fantasy.

"I guess."

"C'mon. What's the one thing you'd order in a fancy restaurant? Like if we were sitting at a table with a table-cloth and candles? And real silverware? And a waiter was standing in front of us right this minute?"

"French onion soup," I say, giving in finally.

I've been craving hot food ever since the first frost slithered into the ravine and took me and Tuff by surprise. And don't get me started on fruit. If only I could get back all the papaya peels I didn't scrape clean or all the mangoes I tossed away before sucking every last juicy drop from the fibrous pit.

Dad always scolds me for being wasteful. "You never know," he says reproachfully. "You never know when you won't have it and really want it."

"French onion soup?" Lise asks.

"Yeah. I wonder if anywhere does it takeout?"

"What makes it French?"

"I dunno? The way they serve it with croutons and cheese, I guess."

"So it's, like, soup made out of onions and toast and cheese?"

"You've never had it before?"

"Nope." Lise shakes her head. "If it doesn't come from a can, you can pretty much guarantee I haven't had it before."

"Add it to the list," I say.

We have a running list of all the things we plan to do together once Dad finally arrives.

"Learn to sail, play a game of chess, anchor overnight by the island, make sushi and try French onion soup. Did I miss anything?"

"Catch a fish and eat it fresh."

"Yes, eat fresh fish cooked in the galley and use the head to take a piss. But be careful not to use more than six minutes of water per day total."

Despite feeling cold and humiliated, I can't help but smile.

Another clattering of coins makes me look up at a woman who has paused in front of us, the toes of her shiny yellow pumps nudging the flattened box we're huddled on. Normally people toss a few coins in our cup and shuffle forward without getting too close and without making eye contact. But this lady is considering us with a quizzical expression.

"Thanks," Lise says brightly.

The lady doesn't speak but our eyes meet and for a fleeting a moment it feels familiar. Then a man is suddenly at her side and they move forward on the crest of the crowd that surges down the sidewalk. This is the theatre district rush that Lise swears makes her more in a couple of hours than she can normally make in a whole day downtown.

It doesn't take long for the stream of people to thin until there's only a trickle of theatre employees straggling home after a long evening. Lise and I fold up our cardboard and tuck it behind a Dumpster in the alley. Then, with the blanket draped over her neck and the coffee cup rattling in her jacket pocket, we head east toward the ravine.

"You wanna get something before we go back to camp?" Lise asks. "I mean, I know you've got your tuna and crackers, but we did good tonight. We can afford a couple of subs."

"A hot pizza sub sounds good."

"Let's hit a Subway, then. It's not the fancy soup you were hoping for, but still, it's something hot and we can warm up while we eat."

∗   ∗   ∗

On the way back to camp, Lise and I make a pact, sort of. She promises to spend another cold night in the ravine with me if I give her shelter a try.

"Just for one night. Just to see how it goes."

I grunt a response that can't technically be considered a *yes* but doesn't come across as a *no*, either.

"Listen, I've just done a week straight Harbour-style and it's been cold as shit. The least you can do is one night, one measly night, Lise-style."

Again, I grunt ambiguously.

"In case you think you're being clever, you're not. You're making it sound like you're saying yes but you probably have your fingers crossed behind your back or some other stupid thing so you can back out tomorrow."

"Whatever," I say into my hoodie, which I've pulled up around my face to conserve the heat from my breath.

The farther we descend into the ravine the darker and colder it gets. It's a damp cold that seeps under my clothing and wraps itself like seaweed around my bones;

the clinging kind of cold that takes forever to shake. As soon as we get to camp, we head straight for our sleeping bags, the ones I bought in the summer before the credit card got declined. Lise snuggles deep into hers and calls Tuff to lie between us for more heat. I climb into mine and shiver myself warm.

"It's going to feel good to sleep in a bed again tomorrow," she muses in the darkness. From the sound of her voice I can tell she's lying on her back and from experience I know that only her face is exposed to the frosty air.

"It's only been a week," I remind her.

"I'm not as hard core as you. I only ever sleep out a night or two. I like being warm. And clean."

"I'm clean. I had a good wash at Subway."

She ignores my comment and leaves me wondering if I've started to smell bad, the way I notice some of the other people who hang out on the streets do. Frankie and Josh smelled like sweat and alcohol. What else could I smell like besides dog fur and smoke? I mean, I live in a tent with a long-haired dog, I haven't showered in weeks, and we've had more campfires since the weather's turned cooler. I give myself a sniff but can't detect much beyond the smell of smoke hanging in my hair.

"Do you have enough battery left for a song?" Lise asks.

"Sure, which one?"

"Do you have any I haven't heard before?"

I run through the songs in my head and pull out my phone.

"This was from last spring. We had to get up early so we could move the boat before the tide went out and there was this amazing sunrise. It was rough as hell for two days after, but it was a great morning."

I hold up my phone and we lean our heads together. A beautiful red sunrise appears and offscreen Dad starts to strum his ukulele. He plays a few bars then breaks into a jazzy version of "Here Comes the Sun."

"I love this song!" Lise says and hums along. She has a natural singing voice, deep and gritty, which is going to make Dad gush with pleasure when he finds out. I'm remarkably unmusical.

After a few stanzas the camera moves off the cloud-streaked sunset and onto Dad's smiling face. His beard is thick and grey and his hair long and wild, but his eyes sparkle like stars. I love the way he sings the chorus, all flashy and fun with an extra round of "do, do, do, do." He finishes the song with a flourish, then blows a kiss into the wind. He's such a drama queen.

When I zip my phone into the pocket of my hoodie, the ravine seems quieter and darker than before and I have to swallow twice to control the hot lump in my throat. Neither of us comments on the song and Tuff sighs. An animal rustles in the dead leaves a few metres up the ravine. Lise tenses.

"It's probably just a raccoon," I try to reassure her and remember the panic I felt my first few nights camping out. I barely slept the first week and jumped at every nearby sound, afraid I was about to be attacked by a knife-wielding lunatic, eaten by a rabid bear, or trampled by a moose. I wasn't even sure which option I preferred. It wasn't until I looked up Canadian crime statistics in the library and researched wildlife in Toronto that I realized I was more likely to die from a falling airplane.

"So, tomorrow night … you're not going to back out. Right?"

I roll my eyes in the dark, wishing she'd drop the whole shelter thing altogether. When I don't respond she prompts me.

"Harbour, I know you're not asleep. Just tell me you're going to try the shelter."

"Okay. I'm going to give it a try," I say, even though my heart starts to race.

"No last-minute excuses. Right?"

"Right."

"We'll drop Tuff off with Frankie and Josh at about six, hit the sidewalk outside the theatre for an hour, then head to the shelter just before they close the doors at eight."

"Are you sure? You'll miss the after-show rush. That could be another twenty or thirty dollars."

"Harbour!" Lise's tone is stern.

"I still don't know about leaving Tuff with those guys," I say. My head has started to pound in time to my amplified heartbeat.

"Oh my God! You're impossible! You promised to give Frankie and Josh a try. I know it's hard to leave Tuff, but I bet on my life that they can take care of him for one night. And you won't owe them any favours in return, unlike some other guys we know."

"It didn't seem so, I don't know, *impossible*, when we talked about it before. I haven't spent a night without him before."

"I understand you're afraid to be away from him. But I promise you he'll be fine." Her tone softens and it makes my stomach ache to hear the concern in her voice. "You know I love Tuff almost as much as you do. Would I put him in a dangerous situation?"

"I guess not." My voice comes out small in the darkness.

"I know those guys drink too much, but they wouldn't hurt Tuff. They wouldn't. Besides, he's smart enough to stay out of the way if they start acting up. Look at the time he got their dinner and they didn't even realize what happened."

"It's not Tuff I'm worried about."

"I'll be with you at the shelter the whole time. We can share a room. I won't leave your side. Except maybe in the shower. I promise you'll be safe there. Cross my heart and hope to die. You'll be perfectly fine. And you can charge your phone. You won't have to spend half the morning in the library."

"I like the library."

"I know, but still. It'll give us a morning to do something different."

"Like what?"

"I dunno. Sneak on the ferry and go out to the island. Would you like that?"

Going out to the island sounds nice. I've been craving the wide-open sky almost as much as I've been craving hot meals. But still, the thought of sleeping in the shelter with so many people terrifies me. I've never even been to a sleepover.

"What if they find out I'm not old enough?"

"What do you mean?"

Her question gets swallowed by the blackness.

"Frankie told me you have to be sixteen to stay there."

"You're not sixteen?"

"No."

"Then how old are you?"

"Fourteen."

"Shit, Harbour! You're only fourteen? What's wrong with your dad sending you up here on your own?"

"I'm mature for my age," I say defensively because I am too afraid to admit to anyone, even Lise, that I've been wondering the same thing myself for weeks now.

"True. But still. Sometimes I wonder about him."

"He raised me to be independent and I'm doing fine, right?" I find my stride and keep going as much to convince myself as Lise. "Besides, he's going to be here any day now, which makes the whole shelter discussion redundant."

"So you keep saying."

I'm glad for the cover of darkness so Lise can't see my temper spike. I breathe through the anger, but my tone is still tainted when I finally speak.

"He probably got behind schedule because of that hurricane. Nobody can motor through a hurricane, you know, even on the Intracoastal Waterway. It was probably safer for me to be here than sailing through that."

"I guess so."

"So I can't go to the shelter, right? Because of my age?" I say hopefully.

"Nice try. Tell them you're sixteen. Use the same birth date, but make it two years earlier. You can't tell anyone your real age if they ask. You got that? If anyone finds out you're only fourteen they'll definitely call Children's Aid. They won't care that you're expecting your dad any day. And I don't think very many foster homes take dogs."

*   *   *

The thunder is directly overhead and sounds like a truckload of boulders being dumped beside the tent. I sit up before I'm fully awake, and when a flash of lightning illuminates the tent, I see Lise is awake, too, lying on her side in her sleeping bag. Tuff is still between us with his head resting on his front paws. He whines slightly when the thunder clashes, but he doesn't move or ask to be let out.

"It's been rumbling for half an hour," Lise says above the sound of the rain drumming on the fly. "I'm surprised you slept this long."

I don't answer. I can't find any words or feel anything beyond terror. Despite the cold, I start to sweat, and the panic in my chest swells every time the ground shakes. I squeeze my eyes tight and stuff my fingers deep into my ears. I hum as loudly as I can. My throat tightens and I rock my body as a way to control my breathing. Backward. *Inhale.* Forward. *Exhale.* I repeat this mantra inside my head as if it has the power to keep me safe.

Images of other stormy nights sneak behind my eyelids, but I push them away. *I'm in the ravine*, I remind myself. *I'm safe in a tent with Lise and Tuff.* Despite my efforts, a crash of thunder breaks through and I shudder. I can almost feel waves lapping at my toes and the ocean rising to swallow me.

I feel Lise pulling on my wrists, but I resist her strength. Next, she shakes my shoulders. I can tell she's screaming at me, but I can't hear any words above my humming. Whatever she has to say will have to wait until the storm passes. If I don't block out the sound, if I lose focus, I'm afraid I'll suffocate.

Tuff licks my face, but I don't reach out to comfort him. I don't dare open my eyes or unplug my ears even when a wet gust of wind whips across my face. I hum and squeeze and rock and am only vaguely aware of being pulled into the storm and across the ground before feeling something thin and wet being wrapped around me and Tuff.

*   *   *

The next time I open my eyes, I see a pattern of golden leaves fluttering against an ocean-blue sky. The thunder is gone and so is the panic. But I'm shivering so badly I can't concentrate on anything else. The only part of me that isn't cold is where Tuff is curled up against my chest. I unwrap myself from the tent fly and look around, but he doesn't move. The camp is a disaster. It looks like a tornado touched down. The tent is flattened and lumpy, soaking in a puddle of muddy water. My belongings are scattered everywhere, lying drenched on the ground as if they got shot down when they tried to escape.

"Lise?" I untangle myself from Tuff and the fly and struggle to stand up. "Lise?"

But even before I begin to dig through the rubble, I know Lise is gone. Why would anyone stay in this soaking mess of a camp? Not only am I wet, but I'm covered in brown leaves. It's hard to move in my wet jeans and my hoodie feels like twenty pounds of armour on my shoulders.

Don't panic. Breathe. One thing at a time, I tell myself as I pat down every pocket and finally find my phone. It's wet, but shows three bars of power, which means it's still working. I sigh. Although everything I own is drenched, I still have a connection to Dad. And I can call for help in an emergency.

I flick to my contacts to look for Brandon's number before I remember that Lise deleted it. *Shit*, I think. There's exactly one person in this whole city who would drop everything and come help if I really needed it, and now I don't even have his number.

"What was Lise thinking?" I complain out loud to Tuff in a ranting tone that makes him look nervous. "Just because Brandon reminds her of her ex, doesn't mean he doesn't have a good heart. You liked him? Right? And you're a good judge of character."

I look around at the disaster again and force myself to think. "What did I do with that flyer for piano lessons, the one with his number on it? It has to be here somewhere."

Tuff slinks away and curls up in a patch of sunshine with his nose tucked under his tail. I watch him enviously, then start to clean up.

The first thing I do is to wrestle both sleeping bags from the tent. It's hard to do anything over the shivering but I wring out as much water as possible. I use the drawstring to tie one end of the sleeping bag to a tree and then twist the other end with my hands. Coffee-coloured water runs down my arms. I twist until my fingers ache, then I spread it over a clump of bushes in the sun. Hopefully it'll be dry by nightfall. I do the same with the other sleeping bag, then collect and wring out scattered pieces of clothing. I hang everything over tree branches until it looks like I'm living in a refugee camp. The last thing I do is I re-erect the tent and wipe out as much of the mud as I can.

The wet ground makes it hard to walk and when I slip and land on my bum, Tuff glances at me briefly before he closes his eyes and goes back to sleep. That dog has an incredible capacity for being able to sleep through difficult situations.

"Thanks for the help," I mutter bitterly.

I collect the cans of tuna that have tumbled from the mouth of the tent and stack them next to my jugs of water. The paper labels have peeled away, but that's okay since every can is the same. When I stretch out the tent fly, I find the bag of dog food and a tin of crackers under a bush, wrapped in a sheet of plastic. Luckily they escaped the drenching and Tuff perks up when I dump kibble on the ground for his breakfast.

I don't stop to eat, but wipe wet hair out of my face and continue to organize the campsite. If only I could find the lighter I'd start a fire. But it's in Lise's pocket for all I know.

Working in the sun slows my shivering, but since the clothes on my body are still wet, I strip and hang those, as well. I'm taking off my jeans when I find a crumpled ball of green paper in my pocket. I lay it out carefully in the sun and type Brandon's number back in my phone. Somehow having it makes me feel calmer, less alone. Like someone has my back.

"C'mere, Tuff." I whistle. When he comes close, I feel bad for ranting at him. I wrap myself around him and lie down on the driest patch of grass I can find. The warmth of the sun caresses my bare back and somehow I fall asleep. It's not a comfortable sleep, but at least it's an escape. When I open my eyes again, I realize I'm finally warm, but Tuff is gone.

"Tuff?"

A blanket falls away when I sit up.

"She lives," Lise says, deadpan.

I turn to see her and Tuff sitting nearby.

"What time is it?"

Lise glances at the sun and screws up her mouth.

"Probably about eleven."

"Where were you?"

"Getting you a blanket so you didn't freeze your ass off lying naked on the ground in the middle of October. What were you thinking? Anyone could have found you like that. You're lucky it was just me."

"Thanks," I say and pull the blanket tight over my shoulders. It smells mouldy but at least it's warm and dry. I stare at the ground, focus on a patch of soggy wet leaves that have already fallen from the trees and turned dark brown. Lise is waiting for an explanation, but the truth is I don't have one, or at least not a good one.

"I'm sorry," I finally mutter. "I shouldn't have done that. It's just everything was wet. And I was tired. And the sun was the only warm thing."

"That's okay," she says, and her tone has softened.

I look up at her gratefully. She is wearing an army jacket I don't recognize and must read the expression on my face when I wonder about her change of clothes.

"I keep a few things with Frankie and Josh. In case of emergencies," she says. Then she hands me a cardboard coffee cup and a box of doughnuts.

"You've been busy," I say.

"Yep. I pulled in all my favours today."

Lise looks around while she eats a honey-glazed and I devour a double-chocolate. "I like what you've done with the place."

"Everything got soaked last night."

"No shit, Sherlock. You pitched your stupid tent in the path of a flash flood. Like, I'm surprised we didn't get washed into the river." Her tone is rough, but the sharp edge is gone. I know I'm forgiven. For the moment.

"Thanks. For … you know."

"For dragging your ass through a freaking thunderstorm while you, like, had a total meltdown?"

"I wouldn't put it exactly that way. But yeah."

"I get that people generally don't like thunderstorms, but that was a whole new level of hiding under the bed."

"I had a bad experience with thunder once."

Lise looks impatient. As much as I would rather change the subject, I know she's not going to give up on getting an explanation and she probably deserves one.

"When I was younger, Dad would sometimes leave me and Tuff on an island for a day or two. Sometimes maybe longer. The first time I was really scared about being alone and then there was this storm. The wind was angry and the waves were wild. Our tent got swamped and it was just a little island. We had to get up into the middle of some mangroves to stay out of the water. Tuff was freaking out and he couldn't lie down, but there was nothing else I could do except hang on. All night. It was awful."

"How old were you?"

"Nine maybe. Ten?"

"And he left you overnight?"

"Only when he had to."

"Why did he have to leave you?"

"Because he had to run some errands."

"Listen, Harbour. Between my mother and a couple of the foster families I lived with, I've had some pretty awful parents in my lifetime. But none of them would've deserted me on an island by myself in the middle of a storm when I was nine."

"I had Tuff."

"Tuff doesn't count."

"He didn't know a storm was going to blow up."

"That's not the point. What kind of errands did he have to do that he couldn't take you along?"

I don't have an answer so instead I stand up and walk away. I know I can't go far in just a blanket, but I can't stand the way Lise is questioning me. I can't stand the look on her face. I can't tell if she thinks I'm crazy. Or if she thinks Dad is. I walk until I'm out of sight and then I sit down on a log. I hold up my phone and stare at it.

"Ring," I mutter.

Then I say it louder. "RING. RING. RING."

CHAPTER 8

FRANKIE IS OBVIOUSLY stoked about having Tuff for the night. When we arrive, he marches across the overgrown lot to greet us, his limbs jerking like a marionette. Then, while we make small talk, he swipes the hair out of his face and says *right on* about twenty times.

"I wanted to get a dog last winter, but Josh refused, even when I pointed out that a dog would protect us. Like if anyone came along and wanted to mess with us we could get him to attack," Franklin says. "But Josh was all like, *no way, bro*. He said we needed everything we had to keep ourselves fed. Besides, he said those street dogs are too spoiled to scare a squirrel, never mind someone who wants to mess with a couple of homeless bros like us."

I hand Frankie a plastic bag of dog food that has been carefully measured out.

"Don't go eating Tuff's kibble if you get hungry," Lise says sarcastically. "There's only enough for one day."

Tuff sniffs the bag in Frankie's hand and knows something's up. He ducks behind my leg and lowers his head and tail. When I hand over the leash, Tuff outright panics. His eyes dart between me and Franklin and he starts to dance and whine, as if he knows what it's like to be left behind.

"Why don't you take Tuff inside and get him settled?" Lise suggests.

"Sure thing," Frankie says and heads for the garage. Tuff looks at me and resists, but Frankie gives the leash a little tug. "C'mon, Tuff. Let's go, boy."

I point and tell him: "Go with Frankie."

Tuff whines but obeys me, as if his body is refusing the separation even though his mind is made up. We're just climbing through the gap in the fence when his whining turns to yowls. It sounds as if someone is ripping his heart in two.

Unlike Tuff, my mind is not made up and I stop in my tracks. But Lise grabs my arm. She has a surprisingly strong grip for such a slight person.

"You promised," she reminds me softly, but sternly.

Then she tugs so hard I wonder if she's capable of pulling my arm clear out of my shoulder socket. I'd complain if I could, if I could find or even form the words. But I remain mute because my throat has turned to stone: I can't talk, I can't swallow, I can't breathe.

"The leaves look pretty, huh?" Lise follows in a gentler tone. Then, without waiting for an answer, she starts to ramble the way the guy out front of the train station does when you sit too close to his turf.

"Back home, where I'm from, the leaves are way prettier. I think it has to do with the colder weather. Or maybe the rain. It rains a lot out east, especially in the fall. But whatevs, the maple trees look like they're on fire.

I mean, seriously. Candy-apple reds and pumpkin-pie oranges. Whole hillsides just sick with colour. It never gets old. I always loved the fall in New Brunswick, even though it was a bit sad, too, because it meant summer was over and winter was coming. And winter bites when you're poor. Five months of wet cold feet whenever you step outside. Five months of wind whipping up your jacket and down your back. Five months of shivering. God, you've never been miserable until you've suffered through a winter in Fredericton with just a pair of high-tops and a lousy jean jacket."

She pauses and looks over at me, but then rushes back into her monologue. I know she's trying to distract me and I don't care. I don't have the energy to care and worry about Tuff at the same time.

"You have to appreciate the leaves while you can, you know? They don't last long. Maybe two weeks tops and only a few days at their peak. There're a couple days in the middle of it all, when the ground's carpeted with leaves, yet the trees still have enough coverage to turn the whole world some shade of orange. But then it only takes one blustery day and those last leaves start crying down from the trees and flying all over the place in the wind. Then that's it. Then the trees look naked and kinda sad. All scrawny branches and bony twigs like a forest of skeletons reaching up to the sky, begging for sunshine again."

She stops and raises her arms with crooked, outspread fingers to illustrate her point.

"Your camp won't be hidden once the leaves come down, you know? Not like many people will be hiking through the ravine when the bad weather hits but, still, you'll definitely be more exposed."

I feel the blood drain from my face and manage to utter one single, syllable: Dad.

"Yeah, I know he's gonna be here any day now. I get that. But what if his engine broke like completely down and he doesn't get here for another month? You can't sleep out once the snow comes. So it's good that you're trying out the shelter. You'll see it's not so bad."

When we get far enough away that I can't hear Tuff any longer, the lump in my throat dissolves. I force myself to imagine him curled up by the fire or sprawled out on Frankie's bunk enjoying a belly rub.

✳   ✳   ✳

We head straight for the theatre district and drag our squares of cardboard from behind the Dumpster. Then we sit, and for an hour I pretend I don't exist. Instead I count the seconds in my head, then the minutes. When I get through thirty minutes I multiply by twenty-four, which is the time left until we head back to get Tuff.

You can do this, Harbour, I tell myself. *You've done twelve weeks without Dad. You can do twelve hours without Tuff.*

"Where's your dog?"

I look up to see a man standing in front of our cardboard mat. He isn't one of *us* but he isn't a theatregoer, either. I don't recognize him, but he looks like he might work in the kitchen of one of the nearby restaurants. He's not dressed well enough to be waiting tables.

"He's hanging with some friends," Lise says.

"That's good. I was afraid he was sick or something."

"Nope. Just having a night off."

The man holds up a plastic bag. He speaks in a slow, deliberate manner. "I brought him some scraps."

Lise takes the bag and smiles. "This will make him happy, huh, Harbour?"

I nod and mutter, "Thanksalot."

The man turns quickly to leave.

"He'll be back tomorrow night if you want to pet him," I call after the man as he hurries away.

But the man turns the corner without glancing back and I hope he gets a chance to pet Tuff another night. He seemed lonely and I know from experience that Tuff is the best antidote for loneliness. Even though the man will probably sleep in a warm, dry bed, I find myself feeling sad for him and wonder if we'll see him another night. I feel I owe him something in return for his scraps, which are thoughtful even if they would have been thrown away.

Lise opens the bag and pulls out a hunk of burger, then hands the bag to me.

"Looks like some ribs in there if you're hungry. Still a bit warm."

The thought of meat is so tantalizing, I don't care that I'm picking through dog scraps. I pull out a rib and gnaw on it. At least Tuff will get the bones.

* * *

A tall black lady is closing the front door of the shelter when we arrive. She scowls at Lise and me as we scurry inside, then she flips the deadbolt and turns to look at us.

"You're cutting it pretty close, Ms. Roberts," she says with a hands-on-hips tone of voice.

"Sorry about that, Joyce. Harbour here was draggin' her feet."

I scowl at Lise for throwing me under the bus, but she avoids eye contact. Joyce turns to look me up and down.

"So this is the friend you've been telling me about. The one who's been making you miss curfew."

She reaches out her hand.

"Nice to meet you, Harbour. Normally I'd do a formal intake, but I'm late for my son's concert. So I'll let Lise settle you in and we can talk in the morning."

Joyce disappears into a small room off the foyer. She re-emerges and hands me a bundle. I wrap both arms around it.

"Clean bedding. Towel. Change of clothes. Some toiletries. I think you'll find what you need."

"Thanks, Joyce," Lise says brightly.

"And I'm expecting a visit from you, too." Joyce wags a finger at Lise. "You know the rules, and disappearing for a week at a time is not cool. You're lucky I was on days or you might not have a room to come back to."

Lise mutters an apology and stares at the ground.

"Don't start pouting. You know I have your back. When you get this one set up, there's some hot chicken soup and cornbread in the kitchen."

Joyce says goodnight before disappearing. Even though she was coming down kind of hard on us, I can tell her heart is as soft as the inside of a jelly-filled doughnut, and probably as sweet, too. Lise leads me up a flight of stairs, down a hall, and into a room with two beds. She flops onto one of the beds and watches me while I make up the other.

"God, it feels good to be lying on a mattress again. It's so soft. And the top of the tent isn't three feet above my face."

I pull a pillowcase over the single pillow, then use it as a backrest when I sit on the bed.

"And it doesn't smell like wet socks," Lise muses.

"The tent doesn't smell like wet socks."

"It *so* does. And wet dog and tuna. It's kinda disgusting."

I ignore Lise's comment and look around. The room feels like a dormitory and there are bits and pieces of someone's life scattered around: a hairbrush on the dresser, a water bottle on the bedside table, a pair of boots peeking out from under the end of the bed.

"Is this *your* room?"

"Kind of. But only if I keep using it. Joyce wasn't kidding when she said I was breaking the rules. I'm supposed to be here every night. They let me get away with a night out here and there in the summer, but I've been pushing my luck lately."

"I didn't realize you had, like, your own room. With, well, with things in it."

"I told you it's a good place. Now hurry up and let's hit the showers before all the hot water's gone."

Lise wasn't exaggerating when she said the hot shower would feel good. It feels like heaven and I wash my hair three times just for an excuse to stay in the steamy stall. The soap smells like childhood bubble baths, and when

I bury my face in the washcloth I forget I've been living in a tent for three months. After the shower, I pull on the crisp track pants and sweatshirt that Joyce gave me then find Lise waiting outside the washroom. She's talking to a sullen-looking girl with shiny black hair. The girl is wearing the same track pants as me, but hers are stretched tight around her hips.

"I was going to call the fire department if you didn't come out soon," Lise teases.

The girl stares at me, but doesn't show any emotion.

"Relax, Lib. She's cool. Harbour, this is Liberty. Liberty, meet Harbour."

I reach out to shake her hand, but Liberty just tilts her head back slightly and saunters away.

"She's friendly," I say, rolling my eyes.

"She's okay once you get to know her. Lot of people come and go here, so some of the lifers don't bother to make friends."

"Lifer? You make it sound like a prison."

Lise laughs. "I figure someone who's here more than a year is a lifer. Believe me, it can feel like a lifetime. But not as long as it feels living on the streets. A month of street corners feels like ten lifetimes."

*   *   *

I stretch out on the bed across the room from Lise and stare up at the ceiling. It's flat white with a brown water stain in the corner above the window. As I gaze up I realize it's been years since I've stared at a ceiling, so many years that the person who last used my eyes for such a pastime had a fondness for pink princesses and magic unicorns. Where did that person go? I wonder. Was she left behind in the middle of the night?

The room seems so open, the ceiling so high, that I miss the coziness of my forward cabin. I miss hearing Dad walking on the deck above and reaching up to place my palms where the soles of his feet would be. It takes me a few minutes to process the uneasy feeling and, when I do, I'm surprised to realize what I'm experiencing is vulnerability. I feel vulnerable the way a mouse must feel when it dashes across an open field or a fish when it darts between clumps of coral in a reef where sharks lurk.

"Do you think Tuff is okay?"

"I'm sure of it," Lise says and rolls over on her side to face me. "He's probably curled up with Frankie, snoring."

"Frankie or Tuff?"

"Both of them." Lise laughs.

"Do you think they remembered to feed him?"

"Absolutely. They aren't completely irresponsible."

"I know."

I check my phone. The battery is already halfway charged.

"Want to hear a song?"

"Sure do," Lise says and moves to join me on my bed. I adjust my position so there's room for both our heads on the one pillow. "I love all the old classics."

I know exactly which song I want Dad to sing and flick through my videos until I find it. He sang his version one night when we anchored near Stiltsville and the moon was heavy and bright over Biscayne Bay. I filmed him with the moon as a backlight. In the corner of the screen the ripples on the ocean glow silver and beyond that the lights of Miami twinkle orange.

> *I've been followed by a moon shadow*
> *My moon shadow, my shadow*

He sings softly and strums the ukulele with such tenderness I smile, knowing the song is just for me. He looks peaceful when he sings and even with him so far away in both distance and time, I feel warm and safe. When he gets to the second stanza and improvises, though, a wave of sadness washes over me, and I am left heaved over, swamped with too much emotion to process.

> *And if I ever lose my girl*
> *If all her love runs dry*
> *Yes, if I ever lose my girl*
> *Oh, I won't have to live no more*

The tears come rushing up my throat so fast they choke me and my body lets out a long low wail that startles Lise and scares me. It's the same sound Tuff was making when we scurried away through the hole in the fence.

Lise doesn't flinch or miss a beat. She simply rolls over, wraps her arms around me and squeezes hard. I can feel my shoulders being compressed which makes it hard to catch my breath but the pressure relieves some grief as well. She rocks me back and forth and whispers into my ear.

"It's okay, Harbour. I've got you. I'll always have your back."

She squeezes and rocks me. She murmurs over and over into my ear that we have each other and everything's going to be okay. Eventually my tears run dry and my eyelids feel heavier than my heart.

*   *   *

Lise is still curled on her side sleeping when I wake up. It's not a slow rise to consciousness that welcomes me to morning. No. My eyelids snap open and I look immediately out the window to see the sun nudging the sky awake. I sit up and pull on my shoes before I even realize what I'm doing. Then I roll up my clothes, unplug my phone, and creep from the room as quietly as I can.

"Hang on," Lise mutters from across the room. Her voice is heavy with sleep.

I pause and glance back. She's curled in her blankets like a question mark, the pillow squished under her head.

"You have to take the back door if you want to sneak out this early. There'll be someone at the front desk asking a crapload of questions if you go out there."

She gets up reluctantly and rubs the sleep from her eyes. Then she leads me through the silent shelter to a back door that spits us out into an alley.

"God, it's early. The sun isn't even up yet," Lise complains. She zips her jacket when we hit the outside air and I duck deep into my sweater.

"You're gonna give those guys a heart attack if you go busting into their place this early."

"You can go back upstairs if you want. We can meet up later."

But Lise doesn't falter or turn around. She trots at my side a few steps before she finally puts a hand on my shoulder.

"Slow down a bit, Rushy McRusherson. God!"

I don't slow down and she doesn't bother to complain again, though it's clear from her pace that she doesn't feel the same urgency I do.

"The least we can do is take the guys a cup of coffee. Can you hold on two minutes?"

Lise ducks down an alley and pounds on a solid metal door with her fist. I stand by the garbage bins and shiver.

"Hey, Mick, you got any coffee you need to toss?" she yells at the door.

The door opens and a skinny kid in a visor looks out. He smiles and shakes his head when he sees Lise shivering on the pavement. She flashes him a wide smile in return.

"C'mon, dude. You must have a pot that you have to toss soon. If you pour it into a couple of cups with some milk and sugar I'd be happy to take it off your hands. Save you feeling guilty for wasting it."

The door slams shut and Lise gives me two thumbs-up. She stares at the square of sky lightening above the alley and blows on her hands a couple of times before the door opens again. Mick hands her a paper bag and two cardboard cups with plastic lids.

"Mick's good people," Lise says as she hands me a steaming cup of coffee. The heat soaks into my hands and it feels like relief next to the cool morning air.

"Let's share this one and save that one for Frankie and Josh," she says.

She takes a sip from the cup, then passes it to me.

"Coffee and doughnuts will go a long way to making sure they don't kill us for waking them up so effing early."

∗   ∗   ∗

Mist is rising off the lake in the golden morning light and the grass is drenched with dew. If I wasn't so anxious about Tuff, I'd stop to appreciate the beauty. But I don't. I march across the abandoned lots and feel my shoes getting wetter with each step.

"Frankie!" I call out when I straighten up from climbing through the fence. "Josh! Sorry it's so early."

"They're probably still passed out," Lise says from a few paces behind me.

The fire pit is dead and cold when we walk past. It smells like the burned-out boat Dad and I found once in the Everglades.

"Tuff! C'mere, boy."

I stop and listen, but I don't hear a sound. I expect to at least hear him whining on the other side of the make-shift door, but there's only silence and, in the distance, the sound of a siren wailing.

"Tuff? Frankie?"

I move the plywood and step into the darkness of the abandoned garage. A few shafts of light sneak through the corner of window that Frankie uncovered for the summer months and in the dimness I can see both bunks are empty. Tuff is gone.

"Tuff! Tuff!" I scramble outside, screaming his name. The pulse in my temples pounds so hard I cover my head with my hands to keep my brains from exploding.

"Don't worry. I'm sure they just had to go somewhere and took Tuff with them," Lise says.

I'm crouched down near the ground and Lise is standing beside me.

"Where would they have to go at seven in the morning? You said yourself they'd likely still be sleeping. Why aren't they here? Where's Tuff?"

Panic invades my body. It started as a scratching in my chest but now my stomach is heaving and my limbs feel numb. My eyes see everything in double and I feel as though I've lost my sense of balance, like I'm teetering at the edge of a steep cliff. That's when I lean over on my hands and throw up into the long wet grass.

When my stomach is empty, I sit upright, on the back of my legs.

"I'll text Brandon. He has a car."

I reach for my phone but Lise grabs my arm and holds it so tight I can't move.

"We can cover more distance in a car. And maybe Erica will make lost dog flyers." My mind is alive with ideas, sparking like a downed power line lying on wet pavement.

"Harbour, chill! It's okay. They wouldn't let anything happen to Tuff. We just have to go find them. Or wait for them to get back."

She releases my arm and I rub feeling back into it. "It's not okay! It's not. It's as far from okay as it can get. It's a disaster. Dad told me never to leave him. Not ever. Not even for an hour. I mean, sometimes when I'm in the library. But I should never have left him overnight. What was I thinking? I can't believe I let you talk me into this."

I start to cry, then hug my body and rock. The desperation I feel is deeper than I knew was possible.

"They found him. Dad was right. He said if I ever left him they'd find him and take him. Now we're all screwed."

"They who? Who found him? Who took him?"

"The guys who want the information. Them. The agents. The Homeland Security agents. Or the terrorists who pose as them. You can never be sure anymore."

"You aren't making sense, Harbour. Why would Homeland Security want Tuff? Or terrorists? He's a great dog, but I don't think anyone's dognapped him."

"Because of the information stored on the computer chip. That's why they want him. It's inserted under his skin."

"What computer chip? What information?"

"Maybe Frankie and Josh are secret agents. This was their plan all along. They've taken Tuff."

Lise laughs, but when I stare up into her face, her mirth dissolves into fear. I stand up and take hold of her shoulders.

"I have to go. I can't tell you why. If they find you and question you, pretend you don't know me."

I turn to leave but she grabs the back of my sweater.

"Harbour, wait! I don't understand. You're ranting."

With a flash, it all makes sense suddenly: the hamburgers, the doughnuts, Lise taking me to the shelter. Horror fills the hollow of my chest. I turn for one last look at her face and pull free from her grasp. "I have to go."

The expression on Lise's face changes once again, this time from fear to relief.

"Tuff!"

I whip around in time to see Tuff launching himself through the air. The next thing I know I'm pinned to the ground and he's licking my face. Frankie and Josh wander up a moment later looking tired and annoyed.

"Dumb dog wouldn't stop howling all night," Josh says on his way past us. He doesn't stop to talk and heads straight to the garage, disappearing through the make-shift door.

"Sorry. Josh is kinda pissed," Frankie says and yawns. "We've been walking around to keep Tuff quiet. I think he thought we were looking for you."

"Bro, you look like shit," Lise says, then hands him the coffee and bag of doughnuts.

"Whatever. I'm gonna head inside and catch some zees. Been a long night."

"Thanks for taking care of him," I say softly from where I'm still lying on the ground with Tuff. "And I'm sorry it didn't work out."

"Yeah. I hear ya. He's a nice dog and all but he can't stay with us again. Josh wanted to kill him. But thanks for breakfast." Frankie holds up the doughnut bag and coffee cup then ambles away.

We watch him fold in half like Flat Stanley and slip through the plywood opening into the garage. When he's out of sight, I wrap my arms around Tuff and squeeze him to my chest until he stops squirming. Tuff finally relaxes and rests his chin on my shoulder with his nose by my ear. I feel his heartbeat pounding against my ribcage and we lie like that together until our shared panic turns to relief.

"We won't do *that* again, will we? No more sleepovers for either of us," I whisper into his ear.

CHAPTER 9

DAD AND I never stay in one place for long, rarely ever longer than a couple of weeks. We move about as we choose, sometimes anchoring in a hidden bay, sometimes spending a few days in a marina, and sometimes mooring if we find an unoccupied buoy. Some nights when I'm tucked up in bed, Dad motors under the moonlit sky so that when I wake up in the morning our destination is a surprise.

We've travelled the entire coast of Florida multiple times, been to the Bahamas, Cuba, Jamaica, Haiti — to all of the Caribbean islands. We made it as far south as Venezuela one winter and as far north as North Carolina one summer. When I was really young, the first year we lived aboard, we travelled the entire coastline of the Gulf of Mexico, but all I really remember is eating mango sprinkled with chili powder in Cancun and buying shrimp straight from a trawler near New Orleans.

All that moving means I never really had a friend before Lise. Besides Tuff, I mean. Sure, I played with other kids when our paths crossed, like when we stayed at a marina long enough for boat repairs, or when we anchored at a town to restock, back in the days when Dad still went ashore. But I left those friends as quickly as I made them.

My favourite times were when we tied up to a flotilla of other boats and, while the parents drank and chatted about the best places to anchor or what marinas to avoid, we kids would hop from boat to boat, exploring each other's worlds. But I never had a friend who I saw day after day for over two months. And the problem, I realize in the days following my night at Lise's shelter, is that you start to miss friends when they're gone.

This is what I think about to pass time while I'm curled up in my sleeping bag, savouring the warmth I know I won't feel again until I climb back in at bedtime. This is what I'm still thinking about when Tuff scratches at the flap of the tent and I'm forced to shed the warmth of my sleeping bag to crawl outside after him. I gasp when I look up, surprised to find a brand-new world, a transformed ravine. Everything is covered in white — not snow, but frost. Every blade of grass is cloaked in a delicate veil that glows silver in the morning sunshine.

The branches are covered in intricate patterns of ice and the leaves left clinging to the trees are edged in white lace. Even the air looks frosty, like particles of snow are suspended in the muted sunlight.

"Holy shit," I say as the brittle grass crunches beneath my shoes.

Tuff runs back from the forest with his breath billowing in front of him. The cold doesn't bother him, but I'm disoriented. The frost bites at my nose, and my fingers feel numb when I pour kibble onto the ground. The water is partly frozen so I bang the Tropicana jug for a drink.

"This is absurd!"

I pull the youth-shelter track pants over my jeans then put on both sweaters and my raincoat to keep warm. Eventually, after two rounds of jumping jacks, I start to feel heat radiating from my core again.

"Lise is right, we need a plan B. I don't know what Dad was thinking coming here. I mean, it may be safer, but we can't camp out much longer. I don't even know if living on the boat will be possible."

But Tuff doesn't answer. He's too busy scarfing down the last of his breakfast. My mind drifts and I picture the next five months tucked deep inside my sleeping bag next to Dad with just our noses poking out for air. Then I bring myself back to the moment, blow life back into my hands and dig out a can of tuna.

"Even this is going to start freezing if it gets any colder."

I remember Frankie telling me to sleep with my drinking water to keep it thawed, but I can't imagine sleeping with canned goods, as well. I sit down and gouge icy tuna from a can with my fingers. I'm too cold to spread it on crackers this morning. When the can is empty I lick my fingers clean then tuck my hands under my armpits.

"We're so screwed," I mutter.

As the day progresses the sun burns through the foggy morning and brings warmth back to the ravine. I watch the icy patterns on the trees disappear and the frost dissolve on the ground. Tuff rolls from side to side on the damp grass and yelps playfully. The cold morning has brought him an extra dose of energy.

I look around and understand what Lise meant when she said I'd lose my privacy with the leaves gone. In the summer I could barely see beyond the circle of my camp, but suddenly now I can see straight across the valley, at the back walls of houses and garden sheds. I realize just how easily the bright orange fly of my tent stands out among the drab grey surroundings. Far in the distance I catch a flicker of someone cycling along the paved trail, then turn toward a sudden movement deep in the nearby undergrowth.

It's just a glimpse, but I freeze instinctively. Tuff's ears perk up and he starts to sniff the air. Then I see what Tuff smells — a coyote standing, staring at us, his coat camouflaged against the grey tree trunks and dead brown leaf litter.

At first I assume it's someone's dog who's slipped his collar, but when it doesn't move, I know it's a wild animal. I grab Tuff and pull him close, then wrap him in my arms.

"It's okay, Tuff," I whisper when he starts to whine. I think about the handgun Lise made me wrap in plastic and hide under a log. I wish I had it now but it would take too long to retrieve. So I sit still and dig my fingers into the warmth of Tuff's fur.

Maybe we're still hidden, I tell myself. *Maybe the coyote hasn't seen us.*

But despite the lies I try to force down my throat, and although the coyote seems unperturbed by our presence, I know he must live nearby. We've probably been neighbours all summer, and he probably already knows our smells and routines.

Whenever I let my eyes wander, it takes a moment to pick him out again, he's so well hidden in the stillness of the tree trunks. He stares without blinking, a stare that could be considered either hostile or curious. There's one thing for certain, though: he's not afraid of Tuff or me.

Eventually his ears twitch. One rotates backwards as if he's listening in two directions at once. Then he sniffs the air, turns and melts into the trees. My eyes scour the ravine to catch another glimpse of him, a clue about what he was doing, where he was going, if he has any intentions of returning. But he's gone and the forest appears empty again. I'm left with only the memory of his presence and the unmistakable realization that we're living on his terms.

I breathe, finally, but hold Tuff tight to my chest. The feeling of his heart beating in his chest calms my own.

"That was close," I whisper.

Tuff turns to lick me and I bury my face in his fur.

*   *   *

"You're really stylin' with all those layers," Lise calls out when she barges into our campsite a few hours later. "You look like a marshmallow with hands and feet."

I'm not surprised by Lise's arrival. I'd seen her coming from halfway up the ravine, which reminded me once again that my campsite is completely exposed. *If I can count ten houses*, I reason, *the people in those ten houses can also see me when they look out their windows.*

"I'm practising for winter," I say when I look down at my overstuffed torso stretched out in a patch of luke-warm sunshine. For a moment, with the sun on my face,

I was oblivious to the fact I was wearing every piece of clothing I owned.

Lise throws back her head and laughs. "Oh, sweetie, you have no idea. Here."

She dumps a bag of clothing over me.

"The church people had a coat drive for the shelter so I grabbed you some things."

I sit up and sort through the items scattered around me.

"That's actually a pretty nice jacket. I almost kept it for myself."

I hold up a black puffy jacket with a fur-trimmed hood. It looks like something I saw one time on a TV documentary about Antarctica. I stand up and try it on, zip it up, and flip the hood around my head. It feels like looking out from inside a tunnel.

"There're gloves, too, and a hat," Lise says as she helps dress me until I'm puffed up like Baymax. "You'll grow to love these ear flaps."

"Is this fur?"

"Fake fur, but feel how soft it is."

By the time she helps me into a pair of snow pants I can barely walk.

"This is a joke, right? I'm not really going to need all this, am I?"

"That and more," Lise says, suddenly serious. "You're still going to need some boots. And a second set of gloves."

When I begin to feel claustrophobic, I peel the jacket and snow pants off, then crawl into the tent to put them under my sleeping bag. The ground is getting colder every night and the extra insulation will come in handy. On my way back out, I grab two sleeves of soda crackers and join Lise in the patch of sunshine.

"It feels like the sun's losing power. Like a dying battery. It's strange to be sitting in this patch of sun right now and not even feel hot."

Lise pops a cracker into her mouth.

"You're not in Kansas now, Dorothy," she says.

I sigh so deeply Tuff raises his head to look at me. There's no place like home.

Although I've eaten crackers and tuna for ninety-three days straight, I don't complain. If there's one thing living aboard with Dad taught me, it's to be grateful for what you have in front of you.

"Look what else I got." Lise digs an ancient flip phone out of her pocket.

"Does it work?"

"Just for texting. It was an old one of Joyce's. She told me to take it and text her if I'm running late. She's on nights for a while."

"She's got a soft spot for you."

"It's the dreads. She says I remind her of her uncle or someone back in Jamaica."

I take the phone and copy the number into my contacts. Then I type: *Hey, Lise. It's me Harbour!*

Her phone pings and she grabs it from me. "Cool. My first text." She types back: *Stop wasting my battery.*

We pocket our phones and go back to eating crackers, the jug of cold water between us.

"So what do you miss the most? Besides your father and the boat?" Lise asks after a few thoughtful moments.

"Different things at different times. But for some reason, today, I'm missing Boca Chita."

"Boca whata?"

"Boca Chita. It's a little island on Biscayne Bay, across from Miami. Whenever we're in the area we stay there. One time we stayed for a month, camped in the harbour. It's a national park now. But my great-great-grandfather owned it once. My dad, when he was a little boy, used to go over there to visit on holidays. Before the government *appropriated* it."

Lise swallows a mouthful of water. "Wait. Your family owned an entire island?"

"It's just little. But yeah, my family owned it, long before I was born."

These stories, the facts of my life and my father's life, are so familiar to me I never bother to think how they might sound to someone else, to someone who grew up without much of anything and especially without parents. Up until this summer I spent almost every day with my father, minus a few nights when Tuff and I slept on islands alone. But I push those memories out of my head and return to the warm memories of Boca Chita that leave me feeling quiet with longing.

"And the government took it away from you?"

"They paid for it. They paid my great-great-grandfather. And then they took it."

"Did he want to sell it?"

"No, but he didn't really get a choice."

"So they stole it from him?"

"I guess. Governments do that sort of thing all the time, though. Like when they build a new road and someone's house is in the way. They boot people off their property and take it over for the common good."

"So what's on the island now?"

"Picnic tables, toilets, an old stone wall, a lighthouse. It's really pretty. There used to be more buildings, like back in the 1950s. But by the time my great-great-grandfather bought it, most of them had been demolished. At one point it was owned by this big electronics millionaire. He's the one who built the bulkhead around the harbour and the stone buildings. But then one night his wife died there under suspicious circumstances. He sold the place not long after."

"I can't believe your family owned a private island in the middle of the ocean."

"It's not that far from Miami, actually. And it's at the north end of the Florida Keys. So it's not exactly in the middle of the ocean."

"Still, you owned a whole island. Who else can say that?"

Lise pops another cracker into her mouth and chews thoughtfully. I lean back in the leaves and stare up at the sky. I feel like a bug trapped under a bowl. There are no clouds at all, just a pure, unadulterated baby-blue canvas stretching from one edge of the ravine to the other. The sky has been clear for days, which has been nice, except it means I haven't caught a glimpse of Mom's face at all.

"What else do you miss?"

There are so many things I miss about my past life it's hard to sort through them all and pick only one. The best thing I can do, I realize, is to tell Lise an interesting story.

"Snorkelling. I miss the coral reefs and the fish. I miss feeling like I have the ocean to myself and being submerged in the water. My absolute favourite snorkelling place is off Key Largo. There's an underwater statue called Christ of the Abyss. It's cool. You can dive down to it and watch the fish swimming around his outstretched hands."

I sit and raise my arms in the air to mimic the statue.

"It's a good place to see stingrays."

"Stingrays?"

"You don't know stingrays? They're amazing. They fly through the water the way birds soar through the sky."

It's true. I do miss snorkelling and kicking around in the warm, turquoise ocean. I miss the fish. And the statue is my favourite place to snorkel, along with about a gazillion tourists every year. But these details are so superficial compared to the ache lodged deep inside my chest, the ache that catches every time I inhale too deeply.

"Why did you guys want to come to Canada in the first place? If I was from Florida, I'd never leave. I'd be warm all the time. I'd never have to put up with frozen feet again."

I sigh and try to remember exactly why Tuff and I are sitting in a cold damp ravine in the middle of Toronto in October. Six months ago, when Dad first told me his idea, he made it sound fun, like a new adventure. And staying in Florida wasn't an option, anyway. But my stomach sinks with the realization that we've made a huge mistake.

"I can't tell you why. It would put you at too much risk."

"Does it have to do with the microchip stored in Tuff? The one with all the top-secret Homeland Security stuff?" Lise snorts, as if she's just heard an off-colour joke.

"I don't expect you to understand. But that doesn't mean it's not true. People have no idea what's really going on. They go about their lives as if getting a deal on orange juice is important. Or that having the newest iPhone or fastest laptop or whatever is meaningful. If people only knew the truth."

"What's the truth?"

I stare at Lise. I want to tell her so much I have to swallow the words bubbling up my throat. I hate carrying the burden alone, being the only person in the whole stupid city who knows what's coming. I hate knowing I'm never going to feel the Florida sun on my face again, or see the palm trees waving in the breeze. I'll never feel the soft, white sand of the Keys under my toes or watch another spectacular sun sink into the ocean in a blaze of red. I don't know how it's going to work, but I've come to accept the fact that Toronto is my forever home and somehow I have to figure out how to survive not just one winter, but seventy of them.

I shift close to Lise and whisper into her hair. "There isn't going to be a Miami much longer. Or a New York or San Francisco or Chicago or Atlanta. They're all going to be blown up and millions of people are going to die. It's the beginning of the end."

I pull back and study Lise carefully. The emotions shift across her face so fast it's like watching the clouds build on the horizon before a thunderstorm.

"What the hell are you talking about? You sound like that lunatic in front of Union Station. The one with the bugged-out eyes who swears whenever anyone comes too close."

I lean close again, just in case someone is nearby. I don't want to tell Lise, and I know Dad wouldn't approve, but keeping it to myself makes my insides feel like they're being corroded by battery acid.

"There's no such thing as ISIS or Al-Qaeda. It's all fiction. Propaganda. The whole thing is an invention of the U.S. government. Even nine-eleven was just a training exercise. They're going to start blowing up all the cities, every single one of them, one by one. The chip in Tuff's neck, it outlines the whole plan. When, where, how, and who."

Lise stops eating her cracker and stares at me blankly. A crumb is caught on her lip and trembles when she speaks. "How *exactly* do you know this?"

"Dad told me. That's why he sent me and Tuff here. So we'd be safe."

"Let me get this straight. Your dad knows about some government plan to blow up every city in the United States? He's the only guy in the world who has this top-secret information. And the best thing he could think to do was to send you and Tuff to Toronto?"

"He's not the only one who knows."

"So he's the only, what? He's the only civilian to know? And all he does is send you to Canada? Think about it, Harbour, why wouldn't he tell someone if this was true?"

Lise stares at me so intently my hands begin to sweat and I have to unzip my coat.

"Who's he going to tell? And even if there was someone to tell, who's going to believe him? It sounds crazy."

"It doesn't just sound crazy, it *is* crazy. Why would the government blow up its own cities?"

Dad always says people choose to be blind. He says people don't want to see the truth because it means they'd have to change and most people are too lazy or too complacent. I'm suddenly worried that I've made a mistake confiding in Lise, that she's going to be one of those people.

"To make money."

"How does blowing up cities make the government rich?"

"So they can blame the oil-producing countries and call them terrorists. Then they can declare war and take over their lands and resources, and nobody will stop them."

"And who's going to need oil when everyone is blown up?"

"Not everyone will die. People in rural areas will live. And people in Canada will survive."

"This is a joke, right? You're messing with me."

"I'm completely, absolutely serious."

"You're serious that you believe this crap or you're serious that your dad believes it?"

"Both."

"What the hell, Harbour? If they blow up the major cities in the U.S., you're not safe in Toronto, either."

"Why not?"

Lise points south. "You know that big lake, down at the waterfront? What do you think is on the other side of that lake? I'll tell you what — the *United States*. Rochester, Buffalo, Cleveland, Detroit, Chicago, Milwaukee. All those cities are on the other side of the Great Lakes. If they blow those cities up, we're all screwed, too."

I feel my temper rising when Lise makes fun of what I've told her, but I try and keep my pulse from racing by breathing in deep. Inhale, two, three. Exhale, two, three.

"I swear, Harbour. Sometimes I don't know who's weirder. Your dad — or you."

"Neither of us is weird," I say hotly.

I'm so upset I want to stomp down a hall, slam a door, or throw a glass and shatter it against a wall. But none of these options are open to me. When I got mad at Dad on the boat, which happened more when I was younger, I would stomp to my forward cabin, slam down the hatch, and lock myself in so he couldn't come in with his ukulele and sing his apology song. I can never resist his apology song or his big, sad eyes.

"Okay, okay. Relax. I don't think you're weird. Or your dad, I guess. I mean he looks normal enough in your videos. But you have to admit he does some strange things."

"There's no crime in being different. If anyone might understand that, I thought it would be you. You're hardly mainstream."

Lise crumples up the plastic sleeve from the crackers. "Point made. But answer me one thing. Where did he come by all this top-secret information?"

Something shifts inside me and for a moment I wonder why I never thought to ask him this one critical question. Where *did* his information come from? But there's no way I can tell Lise I don't have an answer and instead of telling the truth, I say: "It's a long story."

"It always is with you," she says.

CHAPTER 10

DESPITE ALL THE serious warnings Lise gave me about the approach of winter, the one thing she forgot to tell me about was second summer. So when I wake up one morning in my winter coat and snow pants, soggy with sweat, I'm confused. I claw the sleeping bag away from my face and for the first time in weeks I can't see my breath. My nose isn't cold and the air doesn't bite at my fingers or cheeks. There's no condensation dripping from the top of the tent. I crawl outside behind Tuff and the grass is dry. There's no dew, no frost, no ice on top of the water dish I found in the Dumpster behind the Sally Ann.

"Was that it?" I ask. "Is winter over?"

Tuff cocks his head, the closest thing he has to a human shrug, then barks.

My heart warms at the thought of Lise coming back to join me in the ravine and the leaves growing on the tree branches. I ache for my campsite to be hidden again and spending lazy afternoons lying in the sun with Tuff watching the clouds.

I pick up my phone and text Lise: *Summer is back!*

She replies: *Wont last. Gotta make the most of it. Meet me at the waterfront.*

I throw some supplies into my backpack, hide my tent as well as I can with leafless branches, and head south along the bottom of the ravine. The trail is busy with cyclists, joggers, and people walking their dogs. Tuff trots along happily and stops to meet each dog with a friendly sniff and tail wag. I haven't seen him so upbeat in days. The people I pass also seem different. They've shed their winter coats and scarves. There are more smiles than I've seen recently, more hellos and comments like *gorgeous day today, eh?* It's the kind of day when people would be happy to throw spare change at homeless kids, maybe even a few bills. I don't know what's going on, but the city is happy and warm again, and I feel alive.

I find Lise sitting with her feet dangling over the side of the bridge, the one that spans the little harbour by the bandstand. I knew that's where she'd be without having to ask. There's only one boat left, a lonely yacht tied up to the dock, rocking gently in the soft sunlight. My heart contracts with the enormity of all that I've left in Florida.

"What's going on?" I call out as I approach the bridge.

"Second summer. Comes in the fall like this every year. A few warm days before the serious cold sets in."

"Oh," I say, a little disappointed. I didn't really believe winter could be over, but it was a comforting fantasy while it lasted. "I meant, what's going on today. Why are we here?" I sit down beside her and swing my feet in the empty space below the bridge.

"We should go over to the island while the weather's good," Lise nods out at the lake. "I've never been, but

Liberty has and she says there's a beach over there. And a lighthouse. Like Toronto's version of Boca Chita."

"You got a plan for getting there?"

"I got a plan for everything," Lise says and hoists herself to a stand. "Follow me."

Tuff and I trail Lise along the waterfront. The sidewalks are quiet, a startling contrast to the summer when vendors and tourists swarmed like seagulls behind a fishing trolley. The ferry terminal is equally quiet. There're only a scattering of passengers waiting to depart and everyone stands in a puddle of sunshine.

"What about tickets?" I whisper.

Lise hands me a sheet of paper. "There's a guy at the shelter who's a genius at this sort of thing. He told me exactly what to do. Just follow me."

I'm nervous as we approach the ferry behind a handful of other passengers, afraid the codes on our counterfeit tickets won't scan properly and there'll be a scene. But everything goes smoothly and soon we are on the top deck, overlooking the bow.

"Do you know what a relief it is to be on the water again?"

When Lise doesn't reply I look over. Her eyes are narrowed and her lips pulled tight. She's staring at the water with an uncharacteristic intensity.

"I've never been on a boat before," she says finally.

"Not even a little boat?"

"Not even a paddleboat."

She stumbles when the ferry surges forward and I reach out to steady her.

"Maybe use the railing until you get your sea legs."

She flips me the bird, then leans over the railing. Two seagulls hover overhead and Tuff raises his head to watch. But they don't hold his attention and he rests his nose back on his paws. I wonder if he's missed being aboard as much as I have. I wonder if he misses Dad as much as I do.

The ferry ride is short and soon we're disembarking into another world. I glance at the jagged skyline to remind myself we're across the harbour from downtown.

We walk along a narrow street flanked by mismatched houses. Some are painted in bright colours and abstract designs, but others are clad in the muted earth tones I've noticed are so popular in Canada. Some houses are surrounded by tidy but empty flower beds, while others are huddled on cluttered lots covered in dry brown leaves. Most of the homes are compact by Toronto standards. A few are rundown, and others are trying to catch up to the sophistication of their cousins on the mainland. There's a peaceful breeze and the noise of the city is far away, a faint echo over the water.

"It feels like a small town in New Brunswick," Lise observes.

A lady on a bicycle rides past us, followed by three children on smaller bikes. She smiles and nods in greeting and as I watch their backs they remind me of a family of ducks winding down the empty street.

"There're no cars!" I realize suddenly. "Or buses. Or streetcars. Or horns."

We turn up a side street and study the houses as we walk by. There's comfort in their modesty: front gardens that have been put to rest for winter, wagons parked on front porches, an empty patio swing giving credibility to the island's chill vibe.

"Do people live out here all winter?"

Lise stops and peels off a layer of black clothing. "Some do. The ferry runs all winter."

I look around and think, *this island is a place where I could live, even if it's on land and in Canada.* I let myself imagine what it would be like to live in one of the houses we pass, only crossing into the city for supplies. The silence is seductive. *Maybe Dad would even come ashore,* I think hopefully, *and curl up by a fireplace with me to read on the cold winter days.*

It doesn't take long before the street dead-ends. But instead of turning and following a new street, we cross over to an empty lot covered in untamed grass and naked trees. It feels as wild and abandoned as the ravine, like nobody has placed demands on what it must be, or how it must look and behave.

"There's the beach!" Lise says as we come into view of the lake again and a ribbon of sand that stretches in both directions. Beyond is an endless reflection of blue sky so wide and deep I'd think it was the ocean if I didn't know better.

I plop down and yank off my shoes.

"I haven't been in bare feet in months," I explain as I dig my toes in the sand.

Tuff spies a goose flying overhead and speeds away, barking. Freedom.

The sand is not white and soft like the sand in the Keys, but it feels good to have it between my toes. I shed my sweater and pants and stretch, spread-eagle, in my

T-shirt and underwear. The sun is so hot on my face I close my eyes and imagine I'm in Florida, and that *Starlight* is bobbing on the water nearby. The waves ripple at the edge of my consciousness and I remember a time when Tuff and I waded ashore to explore while Dad scrubbed barnacles off the hull. We had that island to ourselves, except for a few hermit crabs scuttling among rotting coconut husks.

The daydream shatters when a shadow crosses my face. I crack open an eye to see Lise staring down, her face framed by blue sky.

"Wanna go for a swim?"

I sit up. Tuff is already paddling after a flotilla of ducks.

"Won't it be cold?"

"You bet. But we won't get another chance until June."

In a flash she sprints toward the water, flinging a dare over her shoulder and leaving a pile of tangled clothes in the sand.

I jump to my feet and race after her, then stop short.

"Holy shit!" I screech. "It's freezing."

"Don't be such a baby," Lise calls out from where she is already waist-deep in the water.

I've never felt such cold water in my entire life. The line where the lake and air meet burns my shins and my feet feel numb. Lise sneaks close and splashes me.

"Stop!" I scream. "STOP!"

But Lise doesn't stop and instead launches herself toward me, grabbing me around the waist and taking me down into the frigid water until we're both submerged. I glimpse her face under the grey water, her eyes squeezed tight, but her mouth smiling wide. When I manage to break free, I explode into the air, sputtering, sure I'm about to succumb to hypothermia. I scramble back toward the beach, but Lise catches me by the leg and drags me deeper.

"You have to get used to it, then it won't feel so cold," she says.

"I won't feel anything at all," I gasp, still struggling to free myself from her wiry grip.

Tuff abandons the ducks and swims circles around us, barking and snapping at the water.

"Please, let me go. It's too cold," I beg.

But my pleading falls on deaf ears and before I know it she's dragged me out to where I can't touch. I have to tread to stay afloat.

"Just breathe," she says. "Give it a chance."

That's when something shifts and I notice the water does feel good. I've never been in fresh water before. It feels soft and thin compared to the thick, salty ocean. The water is cold, bitingly cold, but slowly the pain becomes bearable, almost sweet, and I feel my heartbeat return to normal.

Lise dives under and I follow, kicking hard and gliding like a stingray through the crisp water. It's so cold my temples ache in response. We dive under again and again, then roll over and float on our backs. I've never felt so alive.

When we get back to the beach we strip off our wet shirts, shivering and laughing while we struggle to pull sweaters over our clammy skin. Then we lie down on the sand to soak up the sunshine. The air becomes still and the heat of the day melts the goosebumps on my legs.

"Canadians are crazy," I mutter and turn my face to Lise. Her dreads are coated in sand.

She smiles, but doesn't open her eyes. "We truly are. Sometimes people cut holes in the ice and jump in, like, in the middle of winter."

"Why would anyone want to swim in a hole in the ice?"

"Why not?" Lise laughs. "It's just mind over matter."

Tuff shakes himself dry, then stretches between us. He rests his head on my leg and closes his eyes. The three of us doze in the sun and listen to the faraway sounds of the sleepy island: a seagull crying overhead, a boat motor droning in the distance, the echo of someone's hammer.

"How did you get up here? From Miami?" Lise asks as I drift into a memory of lying on the bow of *Starlight*, rocking gently on the summer waves.

"Bus."

"How long did that take?"

"Two days. I saw a lot of bus terminals. The border took forever." I remember the gun hidden at the bottom of my bag and shiver.

"They let Tuff on?"

"I said he was a service dog."

"You pretended to be blind?"

"Epileptic."

"That's a real thing?"

"Yep. Dad's idea. Seizure Alert Dog."

"Nobody asked you to prove you were epileptic?"

"I have a medical alert bracelet and I had to fake a couple of seizures along the way, like when drivers asked too many questions. And this one time when some old granny complained about being allergic to dog fur."

Lise sits up. "You can fake a seizure?"

"Oh yeah, it took some practice, but you'd be fooled."

"Show me."

"What? Right now?"

"Sure. I want to see if you're any good."

"Maybe later. I'm not really in the mood. I just want to enjoy the sun."

"You're no fun," Lise complains before she lies back down in the sand.

When we get too hot, we leave the beach and head along a boardwalk in search of the lighthouse.

"Liberty said it's down at the other end of the island, so it has to be this way," Lise says when I question whether or not she knows where she's going. "And anyway, we've got lots of time so we might as well explore."

It seems like we've walked half the length of the island before we finally see the lighthouse poking up from behind a clump of trees. It's positioned away from the water, but it feels familiar, like a piece of home. It's built with enormous stone blocks in the shape of an octagon, with a bright red door.

"So, is it like the one on Boca Chita?"

"Not really. The one on Boca Chita's round and fat. It has a balcony and it's surrounded by palm trees."

There's a metal sign attached to the outside of the lighthouse.

"Check this out. Some guy was murdered here back in the 1800s."

Lise wanders over and reads over my shoulder. "I bet it's haunted! Too bad we can't get inside for the night."

We sit on the beach to eat when we get hungry. I pull out a can of tuna and a sleeve of crackers, but Lise groans.

"Seriously, dude, I don't think I can face another can of tuna 'til I'm, like, thirty."

Then she rummages in her bag and pulls out a tinfoil pack. "I told Joyce I was taking you on a picnic and she let me make a couple of sandwiches."

Lise hands one to me — peanut butter and honey — and I almost have an aneurysm it tastes so good.

"I had to agree to be on toilet duty for a week," she complains between bites. "And there're a crapload of toilets in that place. No pun intended."

"Totally worth it." I laugh, but Lise turns serious.

"I had to promise to bring you back, too. She says you can't sleep out all winter."

I hand my crust to Tuff and lick the sticky honey from my fingers.

"Don't ruin today," I say and stand up. I walk to the water's edge, dig a handful of stones out of the wet sand, and try to skip them across the tops of the waves without success.

I look across the lake to where a bank of cumulonimbus clouds is forming in the distance. For now they look light and carefree, but I sense a storm building. I scan the horizon for Mom's face and before long I find her hiding. Her head is turned away from me and she seems to be pointing across the sky. I watch until the shape shifts and her face melts into a new formation.

"We should get back to the ferry," Lise says, coming up behind me. She's tucked deep into her hoodie again. I shiver and notice the breeze off the lake has turned cooler.

We take a different route back to the other side of the island, down a series of winding paths and past monotone grey gardens. There are no flowers or leaves and the shrubs are bare, but there are a series of bronze statues. We pass a turtle and a bear, both upright, wearing human emotions and clothing. There's a beaver, a goose, a rabbit hopping, and even a snail. They seem oddly familiar, like old friends or a favourite cartoon, but I can't remember where I might have met them before. I can't place their faces or a time in my life when we might have crossed paths.

We pass over a bridge and past an inlet before we finally come to a deserted amusement park. The antique carousel seems sad in its stillness, the teacups frozen in time. The Ferris wheel, built in the shape of a windmill, looms empty overhead. It feels wrong to be here, like we've uncovered a best-forgotten secret, and we walk in silence among the children's rides. It isn't right that the train tracks are empty, that the log flume is dry, that the bumper cars are packed away for winter, months from the next crowd of excited children.

Suddenly I want to be back in the city, where the noise and commotion distract me, where survival overshadows thinking, where there isn't the promise of a childhood adventure that might go wrong in one black moment.

CHAPTER 11

WHEN I WAS little I used to imagine what it would be like to play in the snow. I wanted to ride a toboggan down a hill and skate on a lake. I wanted to build a snowman with a carrot nose and a scarf around its neck. I know it sounds cliché, but I wanted to have a snowball fight and catch snowflakes on my tongue. Maybe every kid in Florida dreams of snow, but, during the summer when I was eight, I was so snow-obsessed that Dad broke down and told me about his only experience with winter. I don't know if he thought it was a funny story or he meant to make a point, but it made me double down on my wish. And it made me miss my mother.

Before I was born, he told me, he and Mom took a trip to Colorado for a week of downhill skiing. The only skis either of them had ever been on were water skis, yet for some reason they decided they wanted to hit the slopes. He laughed when he told me how sore they were after three hours of falling down and getting back up. He said they packed it in by lunch and spent the rest of the week reading by the fireplace and watching the snow fall outside. He said they never got off the bunny hill. But he admitted the snow looked pretty hanging in clumps in the boughs of the evergreen trees and that it had reminded my mother of home. He recounted the memory with so much emotion, I think I mistook his tenderness as a reverence for the snow, rather than a memory of a quiet week alone with my mother.

As I trudge along the sloppy grey streets of Toronto in my winter boots, I try to remember why I first fell in love with the idea of snow. Was it a Christmas movie I'd seen? Or a book? Did I meet another child who bragged about making snow angels? Did my mother tell me a story about her childhood in Canada that I held on to? Whatever the reason, I quickly realize the slush covering the ravine and sidewalks is anything but charming. And it definitely isn't picturesque. It's wet, cold, and heavy. I hate my winter boots, and feel blisters forming on the backs of both heels as I walk. But I don't have a choice. My running shoes are already soaked through and stored in the corner of the tent. They might not dry out until spring.

"It won't last. The first snow never does. The sidewalks will be clear again by tomorrow," Lise assures me.

I soldier on in silence. Even Tuff is walking with his head down and his tail tucked between his legs.

"It's not always slushy like this. The colder it gets, the drier the snow is."

Lise is at a loss on how to handle my miserable mood. Even I'm at a loss. I've never felt so hopeless and scared, not even the night Tuff and I spent alone on the island in the thunderstorm. I was too young then to consider what would happen if Dad didn't reappear.

"At least it isn't that cold." Lise tries again to engage me in conversation, but I can't find any words until a car speeds past and sends a wave of cold wet slush across our legs.

"Asshole!" I shout.

Horrified, I stop and wipe the icy water from Tuff's muzzle and back. He shivers and lifts a front paw, and I feel the hot prick of fury at the back of my eyes.

"C'mon. I know a shortcut." Lise tugs me down a back alley and I follow obediently.

"There's a sandwich shop that throws scraps back here. Let's see if we can find a treat for Tuff. He looks like he could use some cheering up."

She pries open the lid of a Dumpster and peers inside while Tuff and I wait.

"Jackpot!"

She hoists herself over the edge and her head disappears.

"There's, like, whole sandwiches in here. Must be left over from yesterday."

Her voice echoes from inside the metal container and her feet kick the air. Tuff must realize something is coming his way because his ears perk up and he licks his mouth expectantly.

Lise lands back on the wet pavement with a cellophane-wrapped sandwich in each hand. She unwraps one and hands it to Tuff. It's egg salad and he sniffs it quickly before scarfing it down.

"He didn't even inspect it," Lise notes.

I'm too shocked to speak, and beyond that I'm angry. Tears pool in my eyes. Lise looks at me as the first ones overflow my eyelids and slide down my cheeks.

"What's happening to us?" I ask in a quiet voice.

Lise crouches down beside Tuff and ruffles the fur around his ears.

"That was a good sandwich, wasn't it, Tuff Stuff? Would you like another? This one is ham. Mmmm. I bet you'd love a bit of ham in that tummy of yours."

Lise unwraps the second sandwich and tears it into pieces, then feeds them to Tuff, making him wait between bites. He licks his lips in anticipation and prances at her feet. Despite feeling overwhelmed, I smile through the tears.

"Tuff's fine. He's not suffering. Those dogs who're tied up all day while their owners are at work, those are the dogs you should feel sorry for."

I crouch down and wrap my arms around Tuff's neck. I fill my face with his damp fur and hang on tight.

"Let me grab a couple more for later," Lise says and leans back into the Dumpster.

A door slams and I look up from Tuff's neck to where a man is standing above us on a second-floor fire escape. He wraps a bathrobe around himself to keep out the cold air, then looks down with disgust as Lise reappears, proudly holding two more sandwiches. He pulls a cigarette from one pocket of his robe and a lighter from the other, but instead of lighting up, he opens the door to go back inside.

"Couple of Dumpster divers out there," he says through the doorway.

We can't see who he's talking to, but we hear the reply clearly.

"I wish they'd stop throwing scraps back there. It attracts more trash."

I'm frozen with shame and yet my face burns at the same time. Lise pockets the sandwiches and shoots the bird up at the empty metal fire escape. I'm beginning to realize it's her signature move and I consider adopting it myself.

"Let's bounce," she says and takes my arm. "That guy's a jerk. It's not like living above some sandwich shop is exactly high-class. Besides, he looked like a meth addict."

I stumble through the alley while Lise rambles on. "I mean seriously, he was like, what, forty? And that's the best he can do? We're still young. We're not going to be stuck out here forever. Right? We just need to come up with a plan. Maybe we can get jobs and find an apartment together. Like, until your dad gets here."

"You ever have a job before?" I sniffle.

"I used to help in my uncle's corner store after school sometimes when I lived with my mom. But I mostly just watched what was going on. And I babysat at my foster homes a lot." Lise laughs uncomfortably. "But I got other skills. I'm resourceful. How about you? Have you ever had a job?"

I sigh. "No. I'm fourteen and I've spent most of my life on a boat."

"Yeah, but you're smart. You know all sorts of stuff about things," Lise counters.

"I guess. Still, I'm not sure knowing *stuff about things* is going to land me a job."

"I've heard getting a job is all about networking. Who do we know who might help us get a foot in the door?"

I draw a blank on that question and stay silent.

"What about your librarian friend, Erica? We could maybe put books away or something?"

I picture Erica's permanently smooth grey skirt, white cardigan, and immaculate hair. "I don't know that we're really dressed for a job in the library."

"Let's go anyway and look for job ads. Like, online. Joyce is always telling me I should be working toward something. Imagine the look on her face when I tell her I got a job at Tim Hortons or someplace."

"Maybe Brandon could hook us up with something?" I suggest, although I don't know what makes me say such a thing when I know it will just make Lise lose her mind, which she does.

"Harbour! I swear. If you bring up his name one more time I'm going to suffocate you in your sleep and feed your tuna to the seagulls. Let me spell it out for you. Clearly. So you understand. The only job Brandon can help us with is making us have sex with disgusting old creeps. Okay? Once you go there, there's no coming back. I'd rather panhandle till I'm ninety than do that."

She storms ahead and keeps an uncomfortable distance between us for a few minutes before she slows her pace again so Tuff and I can catch up.

"Can we at least just go look at some job ads?" Lise begs.

For some reason Lise is pumped about the idea of finding a job, but I'm too busy worrying about getting through the day to start long-term planning. I also doubt she could land a job doing anything more than washing dishes. But I wouldn't mind a quiet afternoon at the library where at least I'd be warm and dry.

When we get to the library, I tuck Tuff under a green shrub with a square of cardboard and my sweater to lie on. Then I tell him to stay. He looks sad when we get ready to leave, but I know he's sheltered from the cold and he won't get wet if it starts to snow again. As I walk away, I turn back in time to see him curl into a ball and hide his nose under his tail.

"We'll only be a couple of hours," I assure him. "And I'll come out to check on you."

Lise's mood changes as we approach the front doors of the library. Her bravado drains onto the slushy sidewalk and her steps falter until she's standing still. She looks at the glass atrium beyond my shoulder, then down at the curb. She watches people walk past, then glances up at the concrete-coloured sky.

"Maybe we should go to the shelter. They have computers there, too. And we can get a meal." She pauses, then tries a different approach. "Joyce has been asking about you again. She'd be happy to see you."

When I don't respond, she tries again: "Maybe I should stay out here and try to drum up a little business. There's pretty good foot traffic? Then we could spring for some French fries and coffee?"

But now that we're at the library, I'm looking forward to sitting in a dry, warm cubicle and reading. "Just come inside for a bit. They have novels and magazines. Probably even *People*."

"You're sure they'll let us in?"

"I come here all the time. It's a public place. They can't kick us out for reading."

Lise follows me through the front doors reluctantly with her head down and a slump to her shoulders. I take a quick look at the information counter to see if I need to avoid Erica, then head upstairs to a quiet corner where we can sit together, away from the judging eyes of the other library regulars.

When I go to the bathroom to wash, the face staring at me from the mirror startles me. It's familiar, yet unfamiliar, too. I lean in close to examine myself. I had no idea skin could look so pale and still be attached to a live person. It reminds me of the underside of a dead flounder before its eyes cloud over in death. And I had no idea I'd lost so much weight. I knew my jeans were loose, but my face looks gaunt, especially below the tangle of hair that hasn't been cut in months.

I strip down to my T-shirt, then lather up a handful of soap to scrub my face, neck, and ears. When my skin feels clean, I dunk my whole head in the sink and scrub until my hair is streaming water and the water in the sink is grey. I change out the water, then roll up my sleeves and wash up to my elbows and inside my shirt. I stand on one foot at a time to clean my feet, scrubbing carefully around the blisters. The warm water feels so good I want to shrink-ray myself so I can soak my whole body in the steamy sink. I imagine myself doing the front crawl across the porcelain basin, then floating like a starfish on my back. When I've washed everything once, I start again. But no matter how hard I scrub, I can't wash away the humiliation.

I pull the plug of paper towel from the sink and rinse the ring of grey from the sides. Then I stand with my head over the hand dryer and shake my hair in the stream of hot air, combing it with my fingers. I don't mind bathing in a sink. Years of living aboard taught me how to be economical with water, how to feel clean without standing in a shower or sitting in a tub. But what I'm not used to is people barging in and seeing me, then backing out of the bathroom as if I have something contagious.

"Sorry," an older lady says when she sees me stripped down, drying my hair. Her eyes dart from me to my clothes scattered across the washroom.

"It's no problem, there's another sink," I offer.

"That's okay. I don't want to … uh … interrupt," she says before the door closes and covers her horrified expression.

When my hair is dry, I collect my things, take one last look at my miserable reflection in the mirror and head back to where I left Lise. I promised to be quick and hope she hasn't taken my absence as a chance to sneak back outside. Knowing her, she's already set up beside the front doors with someone's old coffee cup. As I approach the table, though, I see the back of her head and chastise myself for assuming the worst. *She's probably engrossed in some fashion magazine*, I think, *which is an ironic choice of reading material for a street kid who wears only black.*

But as I get closer I see that Lise isn't reading a magazine. She's talking on the phone. I overhear bits of her one-way conversation.

"Where are *you* calling from? … Yes. In the bathroom … Are you serious? … Lise. I'm her friend … Who did you say this was again? … Can you hang on a minute?"

Lise looks up and sees me coming toward her. She points at the phone and gestures for me to hurry. She looks panicked and confused, and that's when I realize she's talking on MY phone.

I leap the last few feet and grab the phone from her hand. "DAD?" I scream. "Where are you?"

A guy sitting a few tables away shoots me a dirty look and I want to flip the bird at him like Lise would, but I don't. My heart is pounding so hard that my rib cage is vibrating and the echo in my ears makes it hard to hear.

"Dad?" I shout again.

Then the world gets quiet, too quiet, and my brain registers the fact that the voice on the other end of the line is unfamiliar. It's not Dad speaking. My mind scrambles to order my thoughts and words at the same time as it tries to make sense of the information flooding at me from a stranger on the phone.

The voice says something about *Starlight*. Adrift. E.D. Mandrayke. An accident. Miami-Dade Police.

I drop the phone onto the floor and stomp hard with my foot. Lise watches me, her jaw slack with horror.

"What the hell, Harbour! Stop it!"

She tries to push me away, but I use the heel of my winter boot to stomp again and again until there are only crushed pieces of circuit board and plastic lying on the carpet.

"Why did you do that?" She hisses when I stop finally, satisfied the phone is never going to ring again.

The guy at the nearby table makes a noisy show of getting up and moving away. He sighs and glares before he disappears.

"They said it was the police," I say.

"I KNOW that. They had information about your dad."

"But it wasn't really the police."

"What makes you think that?"

"Of course they're going to say it's the police to get me to talk. They were trying to intimidate me into giving up information."

"I don't think so. Before you came and smashed the phone they said your dad was in some sort of boating accident."

"That's what they say. But Dad knew they'd try the *it's the police* trick. He made me promise that if a stranger ever called on that phone to destroy it immediately. It's happening. They're trying to find Tuff and me so they can get that microchip. We're screwed if they track us down. You didn't tell them where we were, did you?"

"I don't know," Lise stammers.

"Think. Think! Did you mention anything about where we were?"

"Uh, not the library exactly. I don't think. Maybe Toronto. It happened so fast."

I pull on my coat and sprint for the stairs, even though it's awkward running in boots. Lise calls for me to wait up, but I don't stop, or even pause or turn around. I have only one thought — I need to get to Tuff.

Lise follows me down the stairs, stomps across the vast open lobby of the library and out into the cold, damp day. She catches up to me when I'm struggling to untie the leash with my trembling fingers. Tuff is happy to see me, of course, but I don't stop to rub his ears. I grab my sweater from the bushes and head down the street. Lise puts her hand on my shoulder and I spin to face her.

"What?" I scream.

"Harbour. They said they found your dad's boat adrift near Miami."

I stare at her and blink.

"That's why he hasn't made it to Toronto yet. Your dad didn't even leave."

I see her lips moving, but I don't register what she's telling me.

"Yours was the only number on his phone. They didn't have contact information for anyone else. They weren't even sure who he was."

Words finally stumble out of my mouth as my brain processes what Lise is saying.

"You shouldn't have talked to them. It's *my* phone. I never said you could use it." I'm so angry my voice sounds as sharp as a crow's on a frosty, still day.

"But you've been waiting months for it to ring. And then it did and you were gone. I *had* to answer!"

I've never seen Lise so frustrated. Her eyes are like nuggets of charcoal.

People on the street stare at us as we argue. A group of girls our age stop to watch the drama unfold.

"You had no right!" I shout.

"It doesn't matter anymore. It's done. I answered. I'm sorry."

The expression on Lise's face shifts and her anger disappears behind a cloud of pain. She reaches out to touch my shoulder as I step back. Her voice softens.

"They said he's dead, Harbour."

I shake my head and hold up my hands to stop her from saying another word. I squeeze my eyes and clench my teeth, then concentrate on breathing so I can speak.

"He's *not* dead," I spit at her before stomping away.

CHAPTER 12

I'M SCRABBLING AROUND in the cold ravine, scraping slush and wet leaves from the ground in search of the exact log that is hiding my gun. In the summer the forest looked so shaggy and full, I'm not sure I'm even in the right spot. I stop and get my bearings again. Three paces north from the tree stump and six paces west from the maple tree with the crooked limb. I look up the side of the ravine, then down, to be sure I'm sizing up the right stump and the right maple. But I'm not even sure I'm standing by a maple tree at all. For all I know, it could be an oak or a poplar or some other tree altogether. I'm not exactly an expert in Canadian flora identification.

My gloves are wet and muddy and my knees ache from crawling across the litter of sticks and branches. I can feel the sting on my face from where I walked into a stand of raspberry cane. When I touch my cheek and pull back my hand, there's blood on my glove, which is mixed with mud. I must look like a lunatic.

I perch on the log and kick at the ground. I'm ninety-nine percent sure I'm in the right place, but no matter how many holes I dig, or how deep, I can't find the gun. Why did I let Lise talk me into hiding it?

"C'mon, Tuff. Help me look," I say as I get back down on my knees to continue digging. But Tuff just watches warily from beyond the log, like my erratic desperation is too much for him to handle at the moment.

"Some help you are. I get that you didn't much like it in the first place, but we need it now. I promise I won't shoot it unless it's self-defence," I plead, but Tuff keeps his distance. His eyes never leave my face, but he doesn't budge no matter how much I whine. Why won't he help me? Normally he loves to dig a good hole.

Finally his ears perk up and I turn to see Lise crashing toward us, waving naked branches out of her face and kicking through the fallen leaves.

"Is this the right spot?" I call out. "I triangulated the crooked tree, the stump and the log, but I can't find it anywhere."

Lise drops her butt onto the log and looks at all of the holes I've dug. "You work fast," she says. "Maybe you were a groundhog in a previous life."

I glare at her and she holds up her hand.

"Okay, I get it. You're not in the mood for sarcasm. Yes, it's the right spot."

"Then where the hell is it?"

Lise takes a deep breath and exhales.

"If I tell you where it is, do you promise not to freak out?"

The hairs on the back of my neck turn to daggers and my lungs start to ration oxygen.

"Where is it?" I try to sound threatening, but it has no effect. The more riled I act, the more chill Lise becomes.

"Promise me you won't freak out," she says calmly, slowly, as if there is no urgency to the situation.

"Just tell me where it is."

"Promise me first."

"*Lise!*"

"Promise!"

I slouch in defeat. "I promise."

Lise stands up and positions herself directly in front of me. She takes a long, slow, exaggerated breath and encourages me to do the same by moving her hands up and down with her chest. My heart feels like it's going to explode with anxiety, but the sudden intake of oxygen buys me time.

"Remember your promise," she says and pauses to see if my temper is going to spike. When I continue taking slow, steady breaths, she continues.

"I took your gun to Frankie. He hid it in the garage under his bed. I didn't want you digging it up and doing something stupid."

"What?" I jump up and shout. "You trust Frankie over me? Have you completely lost your mind?"

Lise pauses to consider my questions.

"Now that you put it that way, well, obviously not. But maybe back then I trusted him more. And right now you aren't exactly acting like someone who I'd want to have a gun." She waves her hand across the scene in front of her as if to say: *I present to you exhibit A.*

"My father gave me that gun to protect myself!" I scream. "It was a gift. For my birthday. You had no right to touch it."

I've never felt such a flood of anger in my life and the intensity scares me. I don't know what to do with the excess energy coursing through my body — zaps of electricity followed by bouts of nausea. I lean over and catch my breath, and press the bile back down into my stomach.

I cycle through the same series of emotions until I feel spent, but still cannot bring myself to speak to Lise. When I finally catch my breath, I whistle for Tuff, then head off at a brisk pace. I'm moving fast, but it doesn't take more than a few yards for him to catch up. He trots at my side, looking up at me. I know he's trying to figure out what's happening. He can almost always gauge my moods and provide the appropriate response. Tears require cuddles, happiness calls for an ear-licking. For rage, the best thing he can do is stay nearby and look concerned. Good ol' Tuff.

"Please tell me you're not going down there to get it back? Like, right now?" Lise chases after me.

I don't respond. I don't look at her and I don't slow down. Finally she gets close enough to put her hand on my elbow, but I yank my arm clear.

"Harbour! Look at yourself. You're wet and covered in mud. You have blood on your face. If anyone sees you they're going to think …"

I don't let Lise finish her sentence. Instead I whip around and shout. "They're going to think what? That I'm homeless?"

Lise shrinks away from me.

"I don't care what anyone thinks. Do you get that? I just want my gun back. I want to be able to protect myself when the Secret Service guys come to get me and Tuff."

"I thought you said it was the Homeland Security agents you were worried about."

"Homeland Security, Secret Service. It doesn't matter what you call them. They want me and Tuff dead just like they want my dad dead."

"Please don't get the gun. It's getting late and it's going to be dark soon. It'll be a long walk to the Port Lands and back. You're angry and you could do something you'll regret. What if you kill someone? What if you end up in jail? Huh? What will happen then?"

"At least I'd be warm," I say, just to be stubborn.

Lise continues to follow me south. "What happens to Tuff if you land in jail?"

"You have to take care of him."

"I can't take care of a dog. I can barely take care of myself. And you know I'm not the camping type. I like having a bed at night."

Lise keeps a good pace but I'm moving at such a rate she has to jog every few steps. A light snow starts to fall from low grey skies and I trudge through the darkening day.

"If something happens to me, you're all Tuff has. And I know you won't let anything happen to him. You love him as much as I do." I say this with more conviction than I feel. The truth is that when I look down at Tuff trotting beside me, my eyes fill with tears and I have to work hard not to let Lise see me wipe them away.

*   *   *

The Port Lands also look different in the winter. The tall grasses have been flattened by snow, and the leafy under-growth that once hid piles of old bricks and used lumber is now just scraggly branches. The wind picks up and I pull the hood over my head. Lise was right and I regret not turning around when she begged me to. If I'd kept my temper in check, I'd be in my tent already, snuggled up with Tuff. I might not be warm, exactly, but I wouldn't be so far from the only bit of comfort available to me. By the time I get back to camp, I realize, my hands and feet are going to be like blocks of ice. They might never warm up. I wipe my nose and stop to get my bearings. Lise and Tuff pull up beside me.

"Am I in the wrong spot?" I look around at the desolate brick and block structures hunkered down amid the wide-open, snow-covered spaces. The sky has darkened and the distant streetlights do nothing to help illuminate the blackness.

Lise steps toward the tall chain-link fence in front of us and peers at the pile of rubble on the other side. There are large machines strewn across the lot, along with a mountain of freshly dug dirt and a mound of old tires, broken lumber, and metal barrels.

"Holy shit, Harbour! They've demolished the garage."

My brain is slow to process the unexpected information, but my heart responds immediately. The threat of danger feels so close and real I can barely control the panic radiating from the pit of my stomach.

"I was down here, like, two weeks ago and everything was normal. Frankie showed me the wood he had stockpiled in the garage and everything."

I walk the perimeter of the fence but it's secure and the gate is tightly locked. I pull off my gloves and start to climb, but Lise tugs me back to the ground.

"Don't even bother. Either Frankie has it with him or it's under that pile of rubble. You're never going to find it. Not tonight. Not in the dark."

I slump to the ground and lean my back against the fence. I can feel the wet ground soak through my pants, but I don't care. I suddenly don't have the energy, or the will, to move. Tuff lies down beside me and puts his head in my lap.

Quiet desperation calls for unconditional loyalty.

I rub the fur on his head and feel calmer, despite the circumstances.

"I'm sure Frankie has it. He wouldn't have left it behind," Lise offers. There's an apology in her tone, if not in her words.

"Do you think they got kicked out?"

I imagine construction men in work boots and hard hats, forcing Frankie and Josh from their makeshift home. If they were sober, it would have been a sorry sight. But if they were wasted, it could have gotten nasty. They would have freaked out; especially Josh, who is unpredictable at the best of times. Did they get a warning? Did they get time to pack? Where did they go? In the face of what has obviously happened to Frankie and Josh, the anger drains out of me.

Lise doesn't sit on the ground, but leans up against the fence beside me. "I guess they got told to move along. Hopefully they got a chance to get their stuff out."

"Where do you think they went?"

"I can ask around tomorrow. Someone will know something."

"I hope they're okay."

"Don't worry about them. They're survivors. They might have to hit a shelter for a couple of nights, but they'll figure something out."

"They had such a sweet set-up."

"Oh, come on. It was a dive."

"But it was their own," I say and start to sob.

Lise waits for me to settle down before she nudges my leg with her boot. I wipe my sleeve across my nose and rub away tears with the back of my hand.

"There's no sense hanging out here. Let's get back to camp."

She reaches down and takes my hand, then leans backward to help me up. "You're going to catch pneumonia sitting on the wet ground like that."

Our pace on the way back to camp is considerably slower, even though the air temperature is dropping fast. I'm wet, cold, and beyond sad, but I can't make myself move any faster. We don't take the valley trail but instead walk through the orange-lit streets, quiet because of the falling snow and late hour. People in Toronto, I've realized, stay inside when the short, dark days arrive.

"I've been thinking about something lately," I say.

"What's that?"

"About this one time, years ago, when Dad and I docked at this place for like a month. It was somebody's house, you know, right on the Intracoastal, near Jupiter. Dad said the owners were friends of his and they were away on vacation. They wanted us to stay and keep an eye on the place."

Lise doesn't respond, but I know she's listening.

"We docked there, tied right up to their jetty and used the yard like it was ours. They had a pool so I got to swim in it every day. We even used their barbecue and sat on their patio furniture. It was pretty cool. Dad talked to the neighbours and the guys who came to keep the gardens. It felt like living on land again. Like we did when Mom was with us in Stuart."

When I look up Tuff is out of sight so I whistle and he bounds from behind a row of garbage cans. I lean down and click on his leash. I shouldn't have him loose near the street, especially at night.

"There was a kid next door and I got to play with him in the afternoons when school let out. His name was David. He was about my age and I liked having another kid to play with for a change. Dad didn't mind, but I wasn't allowed to go over to David's house. Dad didn't have many rules so I thought it was odd, but I didn't make a big fuss. Besides, David liked coming over so he didn't have to include his stepbrother in our games. His stepbrother cried whenever he didn't get his own way."

"How old were you?"

"I dunno. Like nine. Or ten. It's hard to remember. It was the year I was obsessed with Pokémon cards. Do you know them?"

Lise nods and smiles. "Everyone knows Pokémon. I used to watch the cartoon on TV."

"I've never seen the cartoon. Is it any good?"

Lise shrugs. "I guess."

"Anyhow, one afternoon a man and a woman showed up in a black car. They weren't wearing uniforms but they were dressed so similarly it seemed like they were. They had on dark pants and sunglasses. They looked out of place for Florida. I was fishing off the dock when Dad saw the car pull up. He came running down to the boat and untied it so fast I didn't even have time to ask what was going on. He threw me on the deck and told me to get below. Then, in like two seconds, we were gone, motoring straight out into the Intracoastal."

We turn onto a busier street and pass a lady walking her designer dog, some sort of standard poodle cross. Tuff and the other dog wag their tails like propellers and do the doggy dance until the lady looks uncomfortable and crosses to the other sidewalk. I feel angry that she doesn't want her dog to play with Tuff, as if he's going to infect them both with fleas or something. But instead of getting bent out of shape, I shake it off and continue telling Lise my story.

"As we left, I looked out the hatch to see if my fishing rod was still on the dock. It was. And so were the man and the lady. She was leaning down to pick up the rod and my little tackle box and he was waving for us to come back, I think. And yelling. But I doubt Dad even glanced back. I felt *Starlight* surge into high gear and the waves slap against the hull. In a matter of five minutes everything changed and five minutes after that those people were little specks in the distance. Dad never spoke about it and I never asked. I didn't even ask after David. But I was sad I didn't get to say goodbye. We'd made plans that afternoon. We were going to sneak to the park to play on the swings. It wasn't far and we thought we could get there and back before Dad noticed. But I didn't get to go after all."

"So you think those were the guys your dad was afraid of? The Secret Service or Homeland Security, or whatever?"

"Yeah. Obviously."

"How do you know they weren't trying to help? Maybe the neighbours thought it was weird a kid was hanging out all day and not in school and called someone to look into it."

I glance over at Lise to read her expression, but she has her head down and with the shine of the car lights passing by, all I can see is her silhouette.

"If they were just some school officials, Dad would have talked to them. It's not a crime to home-school your kid."

"But he didn't wait to find out who they were. That's what I'm saying. Maybe he jumped to conclusions."

"Maybe. But I don't think so."

"Did you ever see those people again?"

"Not the same ones. But there were other close calls like that."

We turn down Amelia Street and I glance in the window of number 9. Even though there are thin curtains, I can see the movement of someone inside and the flickering of a TV. I let myself imagine, just for a moment, what it would be like to be curled up on a couch watching something with Tuff, and maybe Dad, surrounded by warmth and light. Lise pulls my mind back to the cold, dark street.

"And there's no chance at all that your dad could've been wrong?"

Tuff stops to sniff, then pee, on the gatepost before we move on.

"No. I don't think so. Well, maybe. But probably not."

"But you admit it's possible."

"What are you, a freaking lawyer?"

"I'm just saying. Things aren't always what they seem."

"Like maybe Frankie and Josh didn't just lose their place because of some new development?"

Lise sighs. "I'll ask around tomorrow to see if I can find them. They can't have gone far."

At the top of the ravine I unclip Tuff and he bounds ahead of us in the dark. Lise takes out her cellphone to shine it on the trail.

"You got enough battery for that?"

"For a few minutes."

"You good to stay in the tent tonight?"

She glances at her cellphone. "Yeah. I won't make it back to the shelter in time." Lise pauses, then continues. "Listen, I'll leave you this phone when I go. To be safe. You can text Liberty if you need me. Her number's there. But tomorrow night you're on your own."

"Sorry."

"Whatever. You got anything to eat besides tuna?"

"Crackers and dog kibble."

"Sounds like a feast," she says.

After so many hours of feeling cold and wet, the sleeping bag is like wrapping myself in a warm hug. I strip off my wet pants and socks and slide down until my feet touch the end. Lise does the same and we lie on our sides with a flashlight between us, eating half-frozen tuna on soda crackers, while Tuff inhales the pile of kibble I left for him by the tent flap. Then I turn off the flashlight and look toward the top of the tent. It's so dark I can't see a thing, but I lie still with my eyes open, as if I might see things more clearly if I just try hard enough.

"I wonder if Dad really knew those people whose dock we used that time? I think about that sometimes. I know you don't believe me, but I do try to figure out what is real and what isn't. I get that he might have had a different take on things. Sometimes I wonder if I even knew the real him."

"Sometimes I wonder if we ever really know anybody," Lise says sleepily.

Instead of answering, I roll onto my side, pull my sleeping bag over my head, and sob as quietly as I can until I fall into a restless, tormented sleep. If Lise hears me crying, she doesn't let on. All night I dream of reaching for my gun and not finding it, of needing it and being unable to reach for it, of trying to shoot it and being out of bullets. I wake up to another cold grey morning, feeling even more exhausted and defeated than when I finally fell asleep.

*　　*　　*

Winter is less than a couple of weeks old and already I resent its tenacity. I could handle the cold better, I think, if I had a chance to warm up completely. But the best I can do is warm up one hand or foot at a time. Even thinking about the blistering hot August days on *Starlight* doesn't make me feel better. If anything, I feel worse for all the times I complained about the heat. This is what scrolls through my mind while Lise and I search for Frankie and Josh, a task that seems doomed from the start. Even the regulars aren't easy to find on a snowing, blowing sort of day like the one we're slogging through.

We finally track down Travis and Charlene at a church mission. It's down a narrow set of stairs and in a crowded basement that smells of too many unwashed bodies. The ceiling is low and the walls are painted the colour of Peter Pan's shirt. They're sitting at a small, round table with one empty seat between them.

"Hey Travis! Charlene!" Lise says as she pulls off her toque, freeing her black dreads.

"Lise!" Travis shouts and jumps up at the same time. He leans down and wraps her in his long arms, squeezing until she makes a strangled sound. His face is covered in stubble and he's wearing a black toque. His winter coat is draped over the back of his chair. It looks like something from an army supply store and like it's seen a few winters too many.

Lise pats his back, then squirms to get free. Travis sits, then Charlene stands up and gives Lise a motherly hug, pulling back and holding her face for a moment as if they haven't seen each other in years. The whole greeting makes me wonder who these people are to Lise. How well do they know each other?

Finally Lise turns to me. "This is my friend, Harbour, and her dog, Tuff."

Travis looks up from his bowl of soup and says, "Hey." Then he watches me so closely I start to feel uncomfortable. But Charlene smiles at me warmly and pats an empty chair beside her.

"Take a load off, hon. Today's the kind of day you want to eat real slow. Stay in the warm as long as you can."

Charlene has her hair tied at the nape of her neck with a shoelace. It's dull and brown, without a trace of grey, but she's missing two bottom teeth, which makes it hard to guess her age. Her skin is dark and worn like leather and I wonder if she'll ever be able to scrub herself completely clean.

"What's on the menu?" Lise asks, peering into their bowls. Whatever it is, the colour isn't too far off the hue of the walls.

"Split pea with ham. Pretty tasty. Sticks with you."

When I sit down in the chair beside Charlene, Travis gets up to drag a chair over for Lise. He causes a bit of commotion and people at nearby tables stop eating to watch.

"Can you watch Tuff while we grab something to eat?" Lise asks.

When they nod, I tell Tuff to curl up under the table and stay quiet. Then we push back our chairs and go to the front for a bowl of soup, a mug of bitter coffee, and some thick slices of buttered bread.

"Haven't seen you in ages," Lise says when we sit back down.

Although I feel awkward being in a room crammed with so many people and never in a million years expected to be eating at a free food program, I'm pretty quick to start spooning the soup into my mouth. It's far from the gourmet French onion soup I've been craving for weeks, but it's hot and hearty, and it warms me.

"We didn't come over much this summer. Pretty well stuck to the High Park area. But it's too cold for camping out now. Gonna stick to these parts for winter, that way we can get a regular bite and a bed on the cold nights," Charlene says. "What about you two? What brings you here?"

"Actually," Lise says, swallowing, "we're looking for Frankie. You seen him around the past couple of days?"

Both Travis and Charlene look at each other and shake their heads. We're all quiet for a few minutes and I'm left wondering what happens next.

Finally Lise clears her throat and says: "It's just that he had somethin' of ours and we need it back. Like somethin' I couldn't keep in the shelter."

I notice Lise's speech has changed since talking to Charlene and Travis, but I don't comment.

Travis snorts and rolls his eyes and I can tell there's a whole backstory that I'm missing, but that will never be explained.

"Saw Mike a couple days ago," Charlene says after a moment of thoughtful silence. "He tole me their place got tore down and they were in bad shape. Lost all their shit and were left with only the clothes on their backs. Lucky they had their winter coats."

I feel my stomach clench and although I'd been enjoying the hot soup, I have to stop eating. I can barely swallow and it feels as though the contents of my stomach are going to come gushing up my throat. Lise reaches under the table and finds my hand, squeezing some reassurance into me.

"He said they were talking about heading out west. Like, to Vancouver. Where they wouldn't have to freeze their asses off for the next five months," Charlene continues.

Travis laughs so hard he spews his mouthful of soup back into the bowl. "They didn't go to Vancouver. They're too broke to get to Hamilton, let alone across the whole flipping country." He shakes his head at the thought of them managing to get their act together long enough to make a plan to get anywhere and then takes another spoonful of soup before adding: "Hell, they probably couldn't get themselves to Mimico."

"Maybe they went up north to, like, where Josh was from. Temagami, I think he said. Josh was always talking about a cabin he knew about that nobody ever used," Charlene says to Travis. Then, as if to prompt him, she adds: "Remember how he was always going on about spending a winter trapping beaver or muskrat or something? Figured he could make some pretty good money doing that."

Travis laughs into his bowl and Charlene scowls.

"You think I'm making shit up?"

"No, just laughing at the thought of the two of them living in the middle of the woods trapping beaver."

Travis laughs so hard he chokes and Charlene has to pound him on the back before he catches his breath.

"Asshole," she says under her breath. "I should just let you choke to death next time."

The tone around the table turns as icy as the temperature outside and Lise pushes her chair back as a signal to leave. She finished her lunch, but my stomach is still too knotted to eat another bite.

"You ever go see their place down at the Port Lands?" Travis asks me, even though I've stood up to follow Lise.

"Yeah, a few times. Once Josh trapped a rabbit and roasted it," I say, almost in defence of Josh's dream.

"I found that place, you know. It was supposed to be for me and Char, but then Josh crashed one night and we couldn't get rid of him. We had to leave ourselves. Such a dickhead."

I stand awkwardly, wondering how to respond when Lise hands me my coat.

"Thanks for your help, anyway," Lise says. "If you do see them, tell them I'm looking for them."

I shoot Lise a desperate look and she adds: "And tell them it's important. Really important. Like life-or-death important."

"Got it," Travis says with a suddenly serious tone. "If I find either of them I'll personally drag their asses over to the shelter to find you. You still there?"

"Most nights. Frankie knows where to find me if I'm not."

Travis looks at my half-full bowl of soup and then up at me.

"I guess my eyes are bigger than my stomach," I offer half-heartedly.

Travis pulls my bowl over and stacks it into his empty bowl before spooning my soup into his mouth.

"It was nice to see you guys," Lise says and digs her mitts out of her pocket in preparation for walking back out into the cold.

"Awww. You really got to go? Nothing but cold and misery out there," Charlene says.

"We're gonna keep looking for Frankie," Lise says. "He's got to be somewhere. You guys stay warm."

"You, too, hon. Take care of yourselves."

Travis pats up Tuff before we leave and sneaks him a bite of buttered bread. Then we shrug on our winter clothes and head into the cold, miserable day.

I'm screwed, I think to myself. *I've got no way to protect me or Tuff.* For the first time I feel completely lost, like I'm living on borrowed time and it's about to run out fast.

CHAPTER 13

I'M WEARING EVERY bit of clothing I own, yet I still shiver inside the sleeping bag and wish for the hundredth time that I'd bought the bags rated for forty below. I change positions, hoping to find a warm pocket of air and imagine going back to the man in the store to tell him he gave me the wrong advice, that I need the ones warm enough for sleeping on the side of a mountain. I feel like I might never get warm, like my bones are filled with icicles instead of marrow. I call Tuff to come close and when he noses my face in the darkness, I tuck him into my sleeping bag, drag the second bag over the both of us and eventually stop shivering long enough to fall back to sleep.

Daylight takes too long to sneak into the ravine, but I refuse to get up in the dark. So I lie for an hour, listening to the drone of the traffic above. When the tent finally brightens I crawl outside to make a small fire. If I can get one part of me warm, even a hand or foot, I can claim a small victory in the constant battle against the cold. I rip pages from *The Bhagavad Gita* and crumple them into tight balls. I only tear out the pages I've read and try to forget the look of joy on Erica's face when she let me have a temporary library card. It was as though she thought she was saving me, and I feel like I'm betraying both her and Yogananda.

I lean branches around the balls of crumpled paper, pencil-thin ones first, then thicker ones. I don't even care that someone might see the smoke; that's how badly I need to feel some warmth. I fumble with the lighter and drop it twice before I get a flame to light the pages in a whoosh of heat.

It's not a big fire and I won't let it burn long — just long enough to boil a bit of water in the pot Lise brought to me, along with a packet of hot chocolate powder she pocketed at the shelter.

"C'mere, Tuff."

He comes running when I whistle.

I pour half the water into his dish and cover it with my hand so that it cools before he has a drink. The heat cracks the layer of ice on the bottom and steam rises into the air.

"You want a drink?"

He laps at it gratefully, then rolls in the snow on his back, twisting from side to side and moaning with pleasure. I admire his love affair with winter, even though I hate it with an equal intensity.

The hot chocolate burns its way down my throat and I welcome the warmth that spreads through my stomach and into my hands as I grip the pot. I let the fire burn down, but don't put it out. Watching the glowing embers brings me a measure of comfort, something that's in short supply lately.

When Tuff finishes drinking, I pour kibble into the dish and too quickly it's gone. I know I have to get more soon, or else find a reliable source of scraps. My stomach growls, but there's no point opening a can of tuna until it's had time to thaw by the fire. Instead, I munch crackers, sip hot chocolate, and try not to think about the endless day ahead.

*   *   *

Lise has a few tricks for staying warm on cold winter days, which is why I've stopped objecting when she tells me to meet her somewhere. Today, for instance, she texts from Liberty's phone and tells me to meet her at a medical clinic not far from the shelter.

Are you sick? I text back.

Don't ask questions. Just get moving.

So I do, get moving, and when I see her hunched in her jacket, waiting on the sidewalk, I'm grateful she didn't make me go inside alone. She walks a few steps to meet me and Tuff.

"It's about time. What took so long?"

"Nothing. I came right when you texted."

She turns and retraces her steps beside us. "Must be the cold. Makes five minutes seem like fifty."

"Are you sick?" I ask again.

"Sick of the cold," she says and reaches to open the door.

I hesitate. "Are you sure it's okay to go in?"

"It's all about acting like we belong," she whispers.

Lise marches inside, finds an empty seat, and picks up a two-year-old copy of *People*. She settles into her chair and flips through the magazine as if she owns the place. I follow with less confidence and try to take up as little space as possible. She lifts a page close to her face, then shoves it toward me.

"Can you believe Kylie Jenner wore *that* in public?"

I glance at a photo of a dark-haired woman in sweatpants and a baggy shirt. "Who's Kylie Jenner?"

Lise rolls her eyes and flips the page. "Never mind." She doesn't say it, but I know she thinks I'm hopeless when it comes to mainstream media.

I look around the waiting room sheepishly and notice the contrast between us and those around us. The mother with her coughing toddler and the young man in a leg cast are edgy and impatient, while Lise and I are content to be sitting in a warm room. A businesswoman texts feverishly and shares knowing glances with whoever looks her way, glances that speak of the inferiority of everything around her. Even the old couple by the wall, who surely don't have a busy day ahead, glance at the clock knowingly, as if their disappointment in the medical system is preordained.

Every few minutes the front door opens and cold air sweeps into the room with another sick person. The seats fill up steadily until, within the hour, a newcomer stands by the entrance and glares at those of us lucky enough to have chairs. Still, Lise and I sit patiently, flipping through magazines, while Tuff lies in his blue bib at our feet.

As the minutes tick by, I peel away the layers of clothing until I'm down to my shirt sleeves. It feels liberating not to be bundled into so many garments. I haven't been this warm in days and would be happy to sit all winter in the doctor's waiting room if someone would let me. But they won't. It's inevitable that one of the nurses will approach soon, even in this busy clinic.

"Do you have an appointment?"

The receptionist must have drawn the short straw and stands in front of us with a clipboard in her hand. At least she asks politely. I have to give her points for good manners.

Lise looks up, with well-rehearsed surprise. "An appointment? With one of the doctors?"

I fake a coughing fit and Lise pats my back.

"I thought this was a walk-in clinic. I didn't think I had to make an appointment."

"You still need to check in," the receptionist says sweetly. "Just bring your health card to the front desk and we can be sure a doctor sees you."

Lise smiles gratefully and we watch as the receptionist retreats to her glass cubicle.

I make a show of searching through my pockets until Lise says, loud enough for half the room to hear, "Did you forget it at home?"

I cough again and nod miserably, hanging my head in embarrassment.

"Let's go get it, then. We wasted all this time," she scolds as we bundle back into our clothes and get ready to face the cold. "I asked before we left the house and you said you had it."

The old lady looks past her husband and at me sympathetically as we leave the clinic with Tuff.

"It's terrible they won't see you without a health card these days."

I shrug and nod and don't even have to fake the resignation I feel at having to go back out into the cold.

Outside we head south with our heads down and our shoulders turned into the bitter wind. Prickles of snow sting my cheeks, tiny ice particles that feel like a thousand needles.

"Left it at the house?" I say. "You should say apartment next time. I don't think anyone will believe we live in a house."

"Doesn't matter. We aren't going for an Oscar."

We walk another aimless block before we duck into an alley to get out of the wind.

"Now where?" Lise asks.

"The mall?"

"Security will be all over us in like two minutes if we sit in there."

"We could wander around a bit at least."

Lise looks skeptical, but I guess she figures it's worth a try because we walk through the front doors fifteen minutes later. The glass atrium is congested with people trying to stay out of the cold and a security guard traces a path through the crowd. We keep our faces to the ground and take the down escalator. There's no point going to the top levels where the high-end stores attract wealthy customers and two over-layered girls with a dog would stick out like a baboon's butt.

"Too bad we can't try for some change in here. We'd be warm and making dough at the same time."

The lower level of the mall has discount clothing outlets that advertise 50% OFF, BOGO, and STOREWIDE CLEARANCE. No matter how cheap the merchandise is, though, it's way beyond our budget and all we can do is stand at the edge of the stores and look in.

On our tenth pass of the bottom level we notice a security guard following close. I wind Tuff's leash once more around my hand and square my shoulders. If I were alone, or if Lise were alone, it'd be easy to be invisible. But the two of us dressed in grubby parkas and winter boots look out of place next to the girls in high-heeled winter boots and long knit sweaters. Without speaking we speed up and the security guard matches our pace.

"Let's go to the subway," Lise suggests and nods at the sign directing us toward an underground passage.

"And, like, get on it?"

"Sure. It'll be warm and we can sit down. As long as we switch it up, we can ride as long as we want."

The security guard turns around when we take the entrance to the subway. We turn and watch him go, and as much as I want to hate him, maybe hurl an insult his way, or at least toss him an *up yours* gesture, part of me knows he's just doing his job.

"Do we have enough money?"

Lise and I pull the change out of our pockets. We have enough to get two student fares, with some left over for coffees later. We race down the stairs when we hear the train pull up in a rush of wind and squealing brakes. Then we find seats at the back of a car.

"We scored a heater," Lise says, settling herself into the corner. When I sit down beside her, the heat envelopes me and I feel like I've just won the lottery.

People stream on until the chimes sound. Then the doors close and the train lurches forward. At each stop people get on and off and the scenery changes with so much regularity I stop noticing who's in the nearby seats, who's standing, who's texting, who's listening to music, who's holding hands or a cane or reading a book. I relax into the warmth and invisibility and rock back and forth against Lise's shoulder in a sleepy rhythm.

"You wanna try a free lunch program later? Get a hot meal?" Lise asks.

For the past few weeks my time has been consumed with finding the next warm place to sit, the next place to find a meal, when to move on before someone asks me to leave, how to make a buck.

"I thought you hated those places? Too many weirdos and social workers?"

"Yeah, but if we get in and out fast, and keep our heads down, it won't be so bad. Might be worth it for a bowl of chili and some bread rolls."

My stomach churns at the mention of a hot meal and my spirit rumbles at the thought of sitting to eat at a table.

"You know anywhere good?" I mumble the question with my eyes closed and the drone of the train filling my ears. "That place in the church basement wasn't so great."

Lise lists some options off the top of her head: the St. Felix Centre at Queen and Spadina, the Yonge Street Mission, the Out of the Cold program near Eglinton that is normally pretty first-rate, that church in Yorkville that offers all you can eat, no questions asked.

I murmur my agreement as she describes each place and drift into a warm, comfortable, sideways-rocking sleep.

When I wake up, I'm slouched so far over I'm almost lying on Lise's lap. I sit up and look at the forest of pant legs and peacoats that has grown down the middle of the car. Nobody seems to notice that I've woken up. I look over at Lise and see she's also asleep, her head resting on the side of the subway and her hood down over her eyes. Tuff is dozing on the floor, mostly under the seat with just his nose poking out between my boots and Lise's.

There's something unfamiliar in my lap and it takes me a few seconds of waking up before I see it's a child's lunch bag — pink and sparkly with Hello Kitty on the front. As a child I would have coveted it. I'm confused about why it's in my lap, but I unzip it and find a child's lunch inside: a Thermos of tomato soup, a cheese sandwich, an orange, a granola bar, and a note that says in childish scrawl: *I'm sorry I don't have any dog treats but here is my milk money so you can buy him something. He's super cute. Love Hailey. XOX*

Without warning, my eyes overflow with tears.

*   *   *

We ride the north-south line from one end to the other and back again before getting off and riding the east-west route. I watch how the crowd changes as we go in different directions, how passengers look more defeated the farther east or west we get, as if the distance from the business district is directly correlated to the demands of a workday and job satisfaction.

Shared between Lise and me, Hailey's lunch allows us to stay warm and comfortable until almost dinner when hunger drives us to go above ground. We're the last to leave the subway car and we dawdle in the station. People, in a hurry after a long day of work, flow around us as if we're rocks in the middle of a stream.

"You sure you want to go back to your camp? They're calling for freezing rain tonight."

"I like to be tucked in by the time the sun sets. Otherwise it gets too cold after dark. But I'll be okay once I'm in the tent, even if it rains."

Lise looks like she's about to protest, so I hold up a hand.

"I know you're not worried about Tuff, but I am. He's everything to me."

"I know he is. I really do. And it's not that I'm *not* worried about Tuff," Lise says. "It's just that I'm more worried about you."

"I can't leave Tuff. I can't. I know I have to figure something out soon. And I will. But I can't leave Tuff. You know that."

"I do," Lise says sympathetically. "And I hate that you can't leave him, I mean in some ways. I hate sleeping in a warm room on a soft bed knowing you're freezing your ass off all night. But I also know Tuff's worth it."

Tuff thumps his tail at the sound of his name and Lise leans over to rub his head. When she stands up she looks past me, over my shoulder. Her expression flickers and I turn to look. She strides over to the tiled wall and rips down a poster. Then she grabs my arm and pulls me up to the street where the orange streetlights are flickering against the low grey sky.

"What's that?" I ask. She shoves it at my chest.

I uncrumple the poster and read slowly, trying to make sense of what I'm holding. Impatient, Lise points at the headline: MISSING. Then she points at the name of the missing child: Harbour Mandrayke.

I look up at Lise, but am unable to sort my jumbled thoughts into a coherent question.

"What the hell, Harbour! You're a missing kid!" Lise sounds angry, accusing.

"No! I'm not," I stutter.

"It says here you were reported missing almost eight years ago."

"But I'm NOT missing. I mean, I'm right here."

I look down at my body standing on the pavement to make sure I'm not an illusion and that I really exist. Then I shift to staring at the photograph on the poster. It shows a small child, maybe four years old, with an age-progressed photo beside it of what the girl might look like at age fourteen.

"It doesn't even look like me."

"But what are the chances there are two Harbour Mandraykes? And look, it says: *Primary caregiver found deceased. Harbour is believed to have travelled alone to the Toronto area recently*."

The words *primary caregiver found deceased* are like a punch to the gut and I feel the breath leave my body. I gasp at the stark reality of what I've been refusing to admit. Seeing it in print, though, makes it seem real and urgent, at least for a fraction of a second.

"I'm sorry, Harbour," Lise says as if we've learned it for the first time. "I'm so sorry about your dad."

"We already knew. I already knew. I knew. I didn't want to, but I knew weeks ago," I mutter as tears race up the back of my throat and into my eyes. I gasp for breath and put my hands in my hair. I pull until the pain brings me back to the moment.

"Harbour, there can't be two of you in Toronto," Lise repeats. "Not with that unique name."

"I know!" I shout at her. "But it doesn't make sense." I examine the poster and repeat the same phrase over and over. "It just doesn't make sense."

"It says you were last seen in Stuart, Florida."

My brain scrambles to sort facts, dates, places. "We lived there when I was a kid. Before Mom died."

"Shit, Harbour! Do you think your dad abducted you? Do you think your mom's still alive?"

"No. NO. That's crazy. It's them. They're trying to find me." The idea lands solidly in my mind, like an old friend.

I pull the hood of my winter coat over my face and head in the direction of the ravine. I'm walking fast and Lise is practically jogging to catch up.

"Wait. WAIT." Lise pulls the poster out of my hand. "Look at this picture of the little girl."

I stop and stare at the face. I realize it could be me. I've seen other photos of myself as a child and I did look like that — a mane of messy brown hair framing the exaggerated round eyes of some anime character. But I don't recognize the clothes or the setting. I look more closely and in the background there's something oddly familiar.

"Look at that windmill. It's a Ferris wheel."

I hand the poster to Lise.

"Did you guys go to Disney?"

"It's not from Disney. It's from here. Remember that amusement park on the island? There was a ride just like this."

"So you've been to Toronto before?"

"Maybe," I say. "My mother was Canadian. I didn't think we ever visited, though. At least Dad never mentioned coming here."

"It could be Photoshopped," Lise suggests. "To make it look like you were here."

"Maybe. I don't really know. But it's bad news whatever happened. Everybody will be on the lookout for me now."

I turn and grab Lise by the shoulders. But I must be squeezing too hard because she tries to pull away.

"Lise, you have to promise me something!" I say and hang on tighter.

She finally manages to pull free and rubs her shoulder. "Like what?"

"I have to stay hidden. I can't wander around on the streets with you. No more subways or libraries or bumming change on the sidewalk. You have to bring stuff to me. I'll need dog food and crackers at least. Can you do that?"

"But that means bumming enough change for us both. And it's winter."

"I know it's winter. But now everyone will know how old I am. Joyce will know."

I glance down at Tuff.

"If you don't bring us food, we'll starve. We have to get out of here. I just don't know where to go. Or how. I have to think."

"Okay, okay. Don't worry. I'll help. But I can't promise dog kibble and canned tuna. You might have to take what you can get."

"Whatever. As long as it's edible."

I hate to rely on anyone, but Lise is the only person I know in Toronto, so I have to trust her. I mean, Brandon is clearly not an option as far as Lise is concerned, I can't imagine going to Erica for another favour and Frankie and Josh are long gone.

"I'll make this up to you. Somehow."

"I know you will."

Lise doesn't let me hold her gaze. I know she thinks I'm being unreasonable, but I don't have time to convince her otherwise.

"First thing you have to do is tell Joyce I left town. Tell her I left a couple of weeks ago. But make it sound casual, like you forgot to mention it before because it's no big deal."

"I'm not sure why you want me to …"

I know she's trying to understand what I'm planning, but I don't have time to explain.

"Please, Lise. If anyone ever asks about me, say you lost track of me. It happens all the time, right? People come and go? Like we lost track of Frankie and Josh? Don't tell them where Tuff and I are. Promise me. *Promise.*"

"Relax, dude. I won't give you up. And I'll come down, like, every other day to make sure you're still alive."

"Thank you. I totally owe you," I say and then head toward my camp, with Tuff trotting faithfully at my heels.

CHAPTER 14

I HATE THE RAVINE. It feels like a prison. There's no way to escape. I don't have enough money to get a bus ticket out of Toronto and the thought of going up among the city streets fills me with cold, hard fear. My world has shrunk to a few square metres and turned to ice. There's ice in my veins, ice in my water bottle, ice under my feet. I worry constantly about my future and I play a continuous loop of *what if* scenarios in my head, hoping one will lead me to an obvious plan of action. But none ever does. Somehow, somewhere along the way, I've lost the ability to plan and to dream. What's worse is that I don't know how to fix myself.

I pull a square of cardboard out of the tent and set it in a patch of sun. The sunshine should cheer me up, since it hasn't peeked through the heavy cloud cover in over a week, but it's hard to find anything optimistic about my present circumstances. I gauge the time by the angle of the sun. There's about an hour before it shifts too far west to land on my side of the ravine. I sit cross-legged with my eyes closed and let my mind wander. I give myself permission to stop trying to tease an answer out of the thousand questions competing for attention in my mind and ride the wave of each thought from crest to crest without judgment. It's not the proper way to meditate, but it's the best I can do.

"No offence, but if you cut your hair and got different clothes, you could totally pass for a boy."

My mind scrabbles to the surface of reality and I open my eyes.

Lise is sitting beside me and her expressionless face is the most welcome sight I've seen in two days. I'm surprised I didn't hear her arrive, but lean over and hug her as if she's been away for a month. She hesitates but hugs me back, then pulls away and pats my shoulder with her mitten.

"How long have you been sitting there watching me?"

"Ten minutes. I thought maybe you were sleeping."

"No. Meditating."

"Yep, I caught on to that finally. So what about disguising yourself as a boy?"

I nod slowly while I consider the idea. It could definitely work. Without the wild mane of hair, I could look like a boy. I have no curves whatsoever and have always been a tomboy anyhow. And as long as I don't say too much, nobody would have a reason to be suspicious.

"Do you have any scissors?"

"Not on me, but I could borrow some from the shelter, and next time I come down I could turn you into Harold."

"Or Harvey?" I suggest.

"Or Halpert."

"Sounds too much like a last name. But maybe Harry."

"You just need an invisibility cloak and you'll be all set."

Lise hands me a plastic bag. "That's gotta last two days. It's a long way down here in the cold."

I glance in the bag. There's a box of soda crackers, two bread rolls, three packs of hot chocolate powder, two chicken salad sandwiches, and an orange.

"The sandwiches are for Tuff. I got them in that Dumpster behind the sandwich shop. So don't you go eating them unless you want food poisoning."

"It's been pretty cold out. They might still be okay."

Lise shakes her head. "Don't even think about it. I saw Josh eat a ham sandwich from there once and he vomited for two days."

I wrinkle my nose at the thought of Josh puking all over the garage.

"Any sign of him or Frankie?"

"Not yet. It's like they walked off the edge of the earth."

To hide my disappointment, I look down at the dirty trodden snow under my feet. It's been packed down by my footfalls and is hard like ice.

"So what else's happening, like, up in civilization?"

"Same old, same old. Rich people running things. Poor people trying to survive. I spent most of yesterday taking down all the missing-kid posters I could find. They were freaking everywhere. I must have ripped down a hundred."

"Thanks for that." I cough.

"I'm sure there's a hundred more still out there."

"Better than two hundred."

"You're in a glass-half-full sort of mood," Lise muses suspiciously.

"Maybe. I've been thinking, and I'm sure it's a trick them saying Dad is *deceased*. It can't be true. Just a scare tactic. But now more than ever I have to be smart, keep my wits about me."

Lise doesn't respond and instead smashes at an untouched patch of crusty snow with her fist. She hurls chunks into the air for Tuff to catch. He jumps and twists and finally snaps on to one. Then he lies down and chews it into tiny pieces. He looks so content it makes me wish I could be a dog.

"So did you talk to Joyce? Did you tell her I left town?"

"I didn't see Joyce, but I mentioned it to Liberty. She'd seen the posters and was asking about you. She's a total gossip so she's sure to mention it to Joyce. Luckily you never did a proper intake, so you aren't on the books."

The sun sinks low enough that we're left sitting in shadow and the extra bit of warmth we'd been soaking in disappears. I pull the sleeping bags out of the tent and hand one to Lise.

"Can you stay for a bit?"

She takes Dad's bag and wraps it around her shoulders. "A bit. But then I have to go. There's a comic book thing on at the convention centre and it's a good chance to hit up the out-of-towners. It's pretty funny, actually. People walking around dressed like superheroes and *Star Trek* characters. Mostly adults with money to burn."

I climb inside my sleeping bag and pull it up around my neck. I shiver and cough. Tuff sits between us on the cardboard and out of habit I scrunch my hand into the fur on his neck. When I don't say anything more, Lise's tone changes. She seems almost nurturing, or at least like what I always imagined when I invented an older sister for myself.

"How've you been the last couple of days, anyway? I notice you're coughing a lot. Maybe we should hit the walk-in clinic for real?"

I sigh. "I'm fine, but I'm bored. I'm afraid to go anywhere, even along the trail, in case I see someone and they recognize me."

Lise picks up the end of a burned branch from the fire pit and draws circles in the snow beside her.

"I wouldn't worry if I were you. Nobody pays attention to those posters and that picture didn't even look like you."

"Easy for you to say. But every time I hear a noise, I think someone's coming to haul me off to foster care. Or worse." I don't elaborate but wrap my arms around Tuff and bury my face in his fur.

"Let's go for a walk. There's time before I have to go back," Lise suggests. Her eyes brim with concern, which makes me feel worse.

Tuff's ears perk up at the word *walk*. He pulls loose from my embrace and prances at our feet to get us moving. The way Lise is looking at me makes me feel like a toddler going on an outing, but I climb out of my sleeping bag and stand up.

The sun is still high enough in the sky that its rays reach like fingers into the bottom of the valley and caress our backs with warmth. Since we're not in a hurry to get anywhere, we walk slowly, following the trail as it winds like a vein, coiling and bending in step with the Don River. Although there's a foot of snow covering the ground, the air is still and the day feels warmer than a thermometer would claim it to be. There aren't many people on the trail, other than a few hard-core joggers decked out in high-tech running gear, and we step to the side whenever one of them passes. They don't glance in our direction, not even at Tuff, as if we blend in so well with the dried underbrush that we become invisible. I know to some people we are invisible, or they wish we were. But I'm not offended. Most days I wish I were invisible, too.

Lise and I don't speak while we walk. We don't comment on the joggers or speculate about Frankie and Josh. We don't calculate how much Lise can make outside the comic book convention or even think of new places to shelter on minus-twenty days. Yet just walking side by side soothes me. After about twenty minutes, she stops.

"We should turn around. I really have to get back before it gets too late. I'm sorry. I promise to come down the day after tomorrow."

"That's okay. I get it. Thanks for bringing us some food. Tuff's gonna love those sandwiches." I cough.

"I'll stay longer next time. You sure you're gonna be okay?"

"I'll be fine. I need to get back to my reading list, anyhow. I still have half *The Bhagavad Gita* to finish. That'll keep me going for a couple of days." I don't tell Lise about burning its pages. No matter how I rationalize it, I still feel guilty for destroying a perfectly good book.

Tuff tears off after a squirrel and we stop to watch before calling him back and continuing our walk. He stays close for another few minutes before he spots a hawk circling overhead, then bounds ahead barking at the sky. As we round the last bend before my camp, we see two police officers walking toward us. I stop to put Tuff on the leash and try to act as calm as possible, although my heart is pounding like pistons in my chest.

"Excuse me. Do you have a minute?" The shorter officer stops in the middle of the trail so that we have no choice but to talk to him. He's heavy-set and thick-necked and stands with his feet shoulder-width apart, as if he's a recent graduate of cop college and still trying to remember everything he learned. The other officer assesses us carefully.

I wind the leash around my hand until Tuff has no choice but sit right at my feet. Lise steps in front of me.

"Good afternoon, ladies. I'm wondering if you can help us."

Lise doesn't speak, but tilts her chin up in response.

The shorter officer clears his throat. "We had a complaint that someone was camped out down here. Have you seen anything? Maybe a tent?"

I look at the ground and study a dried thistle poking up from a bed of dirty snow. Its geometric pattern makes me want to reach out and touch it, but I avoid the impulse.

"Camping? Down here? In winter? You'd have to be pretty hard core to do something like that." Lise's disbelief is so convincing I find the courage to glance up at the police officers.

"So you haven't seen anything?"

Lise shakes her head. "We went pretty far that way and there wasn't any sign of a campsite. Not that I saw, at least. Hannah, did you see anything?"

She turns to me and waits for an answer.

"I wasn't really looking," I mumble. "How big's the campsite?"

"Not sure. We had a report about some girl living down here and were asked to check it out. There was a complaint about a campfire."

"That seems weird, don't you think?" Lise asks. "Maybe someone got it wrong. Maybe it was someone burning leaves in their backyard."

"That's always a possibility," the taller officer says. It's his first contribution to the conversation. "But we're still required to come down and have a look. You girls didn't have a campfire, did you?"

"We're not really the girl scout types. I don't even know how to make a fire," Lise says, spinning the word *fire* with attitude.

A bank of stratocumulus clouds approaches from the south and I wish I could float away with them. I imagine wrapping myself in the low, grey formations and falling into a long, deep sleep. If I could do that, maybe I would wake up back on *Starlight* with Dad, and escape this nightmare.

The sound of paper catches my attention and I look back at the officers in time to see the shorter one unfold a sheet.

"How about this girl?" He holds up my missing-kid poster and leans closer to Lise. "Have you seen her around?"

Lise studies the poster, then gestures for me to step closer. My instinct tells me to run, to get as far away as possible, but I force myself to shuffle forward and stare at the picture. I swallow hard.

"I haven't. How about you, Hannah? You see this girl around anywhere?"

"Just on those posters plastered everywhere," I say in what I hope sounds like a Canadian accent.

The shorter officer looks from me to the poster twice, quickly. Then he turns to his partner as if he's about to say something. That's when I give Tuff's leash three sharp tugs and fall to the ground. I become rigid and start to shake. Tuff barks and dances back and forth. As if on cue, Lise drops to her knees beside me.

"It's okay, Hannah. I'm right here with you."

I shake and tremble and let a trickle of foamy spittle escape from between my lips.

"Is she okay?" one of the officers asks. There's alarm in his voice and as I shake I wonder if he's never seen anyone have a seizure before.

"She's epileptic. Happens all the time. Stay clear and it'll pass. She must have felt it coming or she woulda fallen and cracked her head open on the pavement."

"Should we call for backup?"

"It'll be over soon. We just have to wait it out. Her mom works nearby. I'll call and have her meet us."

Lise fusses over me as my shaking subsides. She puts her mitts under my head. Then she takes her phone and makes a fake call to my fake mother. She says I had a minor seizure but I'm perfectly fine, then looks relieved when my mother agrees to come right away. When the conversation is over, Lise hands the phone to me. I curl on my side away from the cops and count to ten while fake mom grills me. I tell her about falling but promise I can get up off the ground and walk a few minutes. I try to sound annoyed while Lise wipes the hair out of my face. When I'm tired of the fake argument, I hand the phone back to Lise and pull my hood up over my face while she finishes convincing my mother that everything is fine and we'll see her in five minutes. Then she helps me to my feet.

"Can we walk with you girls? Make sure you get to your mother?"

Lise steps away from me and over to the officers. She lowers her voice and says: "If you don't mind, I think she'd rather not. She gets a little embarrassed, you know?"

I stand facing the ground so the hood hides my face and I keep my hands jammed in my pockets to keep them from trembling. Tuff looks from me to Lise and back again.

"Good luck finding that girl," Lise says, then takes me by the arm and shuffles me south along the trail while the police officers continue north.

I don't know how Lise managed to ditch the police officers, but I'm grateful when they're gone. We walk in silence for ten minutes before we glance back to be sure they haven't turned to follow us.

"Holy shit, Harbour! That was some sweet acting."

She slaps me on the back and I can't help myself: a smile breaks across my face.

"Right back at you. You handled those cops like they were preschoolers. They're probably still wondering why they let us go."

"Do you think they recognized you? In the picture? Is that why you did your whole seizure thing?"

The question sobers my mood. "I dunno. But I couldn't take any chances. Let's get out of here."

I leave the trail and head up the shadowed side of the ravine. We climb over a fallen tree and through ankle-deep snow, but I don't want to risk seeing the police officers again. It takes some backtracking, but we find our way to my camp in time to see a blur of brown run into the naked undergrowth. Lise grabs my arm and I double wrap the leash around my hand when Tuff starts to pull and whine.

"Was that a coyote?" Lise asks.

We walk slowly around the tent and find bits of shredded plastic and cardboard strewn about in the foot-packed snow. I pick up the bag, but it's empty and torn into strips.

"Crap!" I say. "He took Tuff's sandwiches."

I pick up the orange and hot chocolate packages and shove them into my pocket. Lise retrieves what's left of the cracker box and throws it on the fire pit. I sink to the ground and rest my head on my knees.

"Damn greedy coyote," she says.

"It's not his fault. He's just hungry."

"Yeah, well, I don't see you stealing his mice, or whatever he normally eats."

"I shouldn't have left the bag where he could get it."

"Do you have any tuna left?"

I cough. "Three cans and a sleeve of crackers in the tent."

"I'll come down tomorrow. I'm sure I can scrounge something from the shelter. But are you sure you're going to be okay down here? I mean, what's to stop him from coming back, like, in the middle of the night?"

"He won't bother us. He just wanted to eat."

"How can you be sure?"

"I've seen him before."

"Jesus, Harbour. I don't like this. Not at all. I'm sorry. I really shouldn't have taken that gun from you."

I sigh. "It's too late now. Anyway, I'd rather take my chances with the coyote than the cops." *Or worse*, I think soberly.

Lise checks her phone but I don't ask what time it is. I can already feel the air cooling and by the angle of the sun on the far side of the ravine, I know it's well past three.

"Can I use your dad's sleeping bag tonight?"

"Why?"

"I'm going to run and get some more supplies, then join you. I should be back by dark if I get going now."

Without hesitating she heads out along the trail I've worn through the forest and I call out after her.

"You don't have to spend the night, Lise. Seriously. We'll be fine. It'll be really cold in the tent."

She shouts back at me: "I know about the cold, dumbass. I'm Canadian, remember?"

There's no use calling out again. She's walked too far away and even in my desperate state I know shouting is not the best way to stay hidden.

"I don't want her to hate me," I mutter to Tuff. "One more miserable night down here and she might not ever come back. Then we'll be completely screwed."

CHAPTER 15

I'M NOT CONVINCED the new haircut will let me pass for a boy, but I like waking up without having hair stuck to my neck or tangled around my face, especially when I find Lise jammed up against me, and Tuff scratching at the tent flap to get out.

Normally I get up with Tuff, but today I feel too miserable and the air is too cold, so I crawl across the tent and let him out on his own.

"Don't run off," I say, then sink back into my sleeping bag and shiver to recapture the warmth.

Lise barely moves.

"You still alive?" I poke her with my feet.

She moans. "Apparently we didn't freeze overnight." Then she shifts tight against me again so she can warm her back.

I'm shivering so hard I'm not sure I'll ever get back to sleep, but I can't face being outside in the snow, either, so I close my eyes and imagine warm things like black pavement in July and working on a conked-out engine after motoring down the Intracoastal all afternoon.

The next time I breach consciousness, I'm even more disoriented. The tent is empty and Lise's sleeping bag is on top of me. But I'm not cold anymore. In fact, I feel hot and wonder hopefully if another stretch of second summer has arrived. Then I notice my throat is sore and my head is pounding. When I poke my head above the top of the sleeping bag, the cold air hits my lungs and I cough.

"Lise?" I call out. "Lise? Lise?" My voice sounds strained, even to my ears.

There are no sounds outside and no smell of smoke.

"Tuff?"

I unzip the tent flap and look around. The campsite is empty, too. My pulse races seeing that Tuff is not lying nearby with his head on his paws, but I take a deep breath and talk myself off the ledge.

He's just off with Lise somewhere. Lise has him safe. They're probably running errands or collecting some cash. They'll be back soon.

My mouth is dry and my throat feels like sandpaper so I dig a bottle of water from the bottom of my sleeping bag, take a long drink, and then double over with a fit of coughing.

"Shit," I say to the tent. "I'm sick."

All I can think of doing to soothe my throat is making a cup of hot chocolate, so I climb out of the tent determined to boil a pot of water. I break a few sticks, crumple up the last five pages of a novel I never finished, then start to shiver so badly I give up. Defeated, I crawl back into the tent, climb into my sleeping bag, and fall into another fitful dream.

The next time I wake up and half crawl from the tent to look around, I can't tell what time it is or how long I've been sleeping. The cloud cover is so low and grey, it could be morning or afternoon. Snowflakes fall from the sky and land on my shoulders and mittens.

"Tuff? Lise?" I call out a few times. Then I cough until I can barely catch my breath.

Back inside the tent I chip chunks of frozen tuna from a can. Even with the crackers it's not a very hearty breakfast or lunch, or whatever, but it's enough to hold back the hunger threatening mutiny in my stomach. Wherever Lise and Tuff have gone, I hope they bring back something to eat. I don't have the energy to climb out of the ravine and go look for them so I wrap myself in both sleeping bags and wait for them to return. Being sick is disorienting. When I wake up again, it takes me a moment to unravel reality. Is it the same day I ate the frozen tuna, or the next day? Have Tuff and Lise been gone overnight?

There's a rustling sound outside.

"Lise? Tuff?" I call out with a voice as ragged as the old sailor we met one time at Boca Chita. He'd tied up without a permit and bragged to Dad that he hadn't paid for a place to sleep in thirty years. He had to cheat the system, he said, so he could afford his pack-a-day smoking habit. For some reason his face looms large in my mind. I can remember with vivid clarity that his fingers and teeth were as brown as the ground and the skin on his face grooved with years of salt and weather. How long before my face starts to show the effects of living in a cold ravine?

"It's me," Lise says. She unzips the flap of the tent and kneels in the opening. "How're you feeling?"

"Crappy." I cough and sit up with the sleeping bag still around the lower half of my body.

Her hat is white with snow and her cheeks bright pink. She hands me a box of day-old doughnuts and a coffee that's warm and sweet. It calms my throat when I take a sip. I open the box and pick out a jelly-filled.

"Listen, I've got bad news."

I stop mid-bite and wait for the bomb to drop.

"Tuff's gone. He wasn't around when I woke up. I've been looking for him, but no luck so far."

When I move to leave, Lise stops me. "I don't think you're in any shape to be outside walking around. You were coughing so hard this morning I thought you were going to bring up a lung."

"I was coughing?"

Lise nods. "I can't believe you slept through it."

"You're going to keep looking for Tuff?"

"Of course. Where do you think he might be?"

"I don't know. He's never run off before. If he got chasing a rabbit or something, he might have gone in any direction. I've got to go find him."

My stomach heaves when I remember the coyote, but when I try to crawl out of the tent Lise pushes my shoulders back inside.

"Don't panic. It's only been a couple of hours. He'll probably turn up on his own. But I'll walk along the river and see if he's wandering around."

"Shit, Lise! What if he's lost? What if someone took him? I can't lie here and do nothing."

"Tuff's too smart to get himself in trouble. He probably just lost track of time. You keep warm and wait here. You wouldn't want him to come back and find an empty camp, then take off again, right?" Lise pauses. "The phone is in my sleeping bag if you need it."

Lise has a point and I feel so weak I know there's nothing to do but wait and worry.

"I'll be back in a bit."

When Lise leaves I tie back the tent flap and watch the snowflakes drift to the ground. I eat two more doughnuts and finish the coffee. Then I lie back down, with my head by the opening, and pray to God and Buddha *and* Yogananda that Tuff comes back. I close my eyes and concentrate so intently on reaching him with my mind that my prayers melt into a dream where Tuff and I are walking through a forest, crunching over dead leaves. When we stop, silence rises up and takes over. I look up at the sky and search the clouds for Mom's face. It takes only seconds before I see her. She smiles directly at me and I feel happy until I notice a pack of coyotes closing in around us. Tuff tries to chase them off, but I pull him back. There are too many to fight. We're surrounded, trapped, and when I try to scream for help my voice is gone. I can't run and I can't talk.

I wake with a start and see the snow is falling faster and thicker, and the ground outside is covered fresh and clean. How many times can I wake up in one day?

I sit up, but the effort makes me cough and my chest feels like it's going to split open. My lungs scream for air and I hear a crackling sound when I take a deep breath. I know I can't sleep another cold night in the tent. This is the moment Lise has been nagging me about for weeks, the moment we tried to plan for. I need to go to the shelter and get better. I have to find somewhere for Tuff to stay.

Tuff. I remind myself. *Tuff is missing and Lise is out looking for him.*

I dig the phone from Lise's sleeping bag and look at the numbers listed. Although I have no clear idea how long Lise has been gone, I know she's already doing everything she can to find Tuff and I have no choice but try my other contact. I push Lise's warning about Brandon from my mind, hoping she was wrong, or at least exaggerating.

I type in Brandon's number, then: *Brandon? It's me, Harbour. Are you there?* Then I hit send before I lose my nerve.

A rustling sound from outside the tent makes me freeze. Lise can't know who I'm texting so I poke my head outside before she can catch me in the act. And there I see, with a wave of relief, that Tuff is sniffing the side of the tent.

"You came back, finally," I say, feeling further weakened by the rush of emotion at seeing him safe. "It's about time. You had me worried."

Tuff lifts his head suddenly at the sound of my voice.

"Where've you been?" I reach out to rub his ears, but he jerks away.

"Tuff! Come here," I say sternly.

But he doesn't come closer at all. He just watches me warily while I cough.

"Don't worry. Come here. I'm just a little sick."

I reach out again, but again he backs up. That's when I notice he's wearing a yellow collar. That's also when I realize it's not Tuff at all. And that's when Tuff comes around the other side of the tent and starts to lick my face.

I wrap the sleeping bag around my shoulders and climb outside to be sure I'm not seeing things or dreaming. And I'm not. There really are two Tuffs sniffing around the campsite, except that one of them is a girl.

"Hey Tuff, who's your friend?"

I crouch down and the strange dog approaches. She gets close enough to sniff me and that gives me the opportunity to reach out and pet her. She leans into my hand when I rub her ears and although I feel weak and my head is pounding, I smile.

Suddenly the mystery dog perks up her ears. She cocks her head as if listening, then races off. Before I can grab Tuff, he takes off in pursuit of his new friend.

"Tuff! Tuff!" I try to call him back, but the effort brings on another fit of coughing. I cough until I think I'm going to pass out. Then I sit down on a log and cough some more.

"Hello? Are you okay?"

My pulse sputters when I hear an unfamiliar voice and I jump to my feet in time to watch a lady push back the branches and step into my clearing. She's wearing a long black coat, a grey hat, and a yellow scarf. She is holding a dog leash and looks around my camp cautiously, at me with open curiosity and a measure of confusion.

"Hi," I say and swallow the beginning of another cough.

"Is this your dog?"

Tuff is following close behind his friend, who is once more vacuuming up every smell in my campsite.

I nod, then ask: "Is that *your* dog?"

The lady stares at me and, when I speak, her eyes narrow. I realize my mistake too late and chastise myself for not trying to sound more like a boy — a Canadian boy. I reach up to rub the back of my head and breathe easier when I feel of the stubble of my new haircut. Even if I can't pull off the boy disguise, I definitely look nothing like the age-progressed photo on the missing-kid poster. The lady looks at Tuff and her dog, then back at me.

"Harbour?"

In an instant, panic floods my limbs. They feel fluid. At the same time the blood pumping through my heart freezes. I step backwards and glance around quickly like a trapped animal. Surely I can outrun a middle-aged lady in a long coat, even in my weakened state.

"Is that Tuff Stuff?"

My mind scrambles to remember everything about the missing-kid poster. Did it say anything about Tuff?

"You're Harbour, aren't you? Harbour Mandrayke?"

I know I should deny it, go with the new identity Lise created for me. I should claim to be Hayden Miller. But I can't. When faced with a stranger accusing me of being Harbour Mandrayke, all I can do is nod.

"I can't believe you still have Tuff. No wonder he ended up in my yard."

I have no idea what the lady is talking about and I'm expecting Lise to appear any second to explain, but when I scan the forest there's no sign of movement.

"Do you know Lise?" I ask finally.

The lady shakes her head. "No, I'm sorry. I don't know anyone named Lise. Should I?"

"I don't know. I don't know where she went. She should be back soon."

"Is Lise your friend?"

I nod, and cough.

"You're sick. You poor thing. You can't stay down here in this tent. It's a wonder you don't have pneumonia. Come on, let's get you into a warm bed and get some hot fluids into you."

The lady steps toward me and I stumble backward. Alarms go off in my head and the need to flee is so strong I feel it pulling my feet down the side of the ravine to safety.

"Wait!" The lady says sharply, and for some reason my body obeys. "You don't recognize me, do you?"

I stare at the lady. Even though she seems friendly, and maybe familiar, I haven't a clue who she might be or what she's doing in my camp.

"Harbour, I'm your aunt. Your mother's sister."

My brain is trying so hard to make sense of what's happening, it screams with the effort of lining up memories, pieces of information from my past and the lady standing before me. When I look close I can see a resemblance to my mother. Even from under her hat, I see she has the same dark, wild hair as my mother, the untameable hair I had myself until the day before yesterday. She has the same narrow chin and thick, black eyelashes. But I don't believe in fairy tales and happy endings. I don't have an aunt. It's impossible. It's a set-up. My brain scans through all the warnings and scenarios Dad put me through over the years.

"What do you do if an adult approaches you and asks why you're alone?"

"Point to an adult and say, 'That's my dad over there.'"

"Good. And what do you do if you meet someone who says I sent them to get you?"

"Ask for the code word."

"What's the code word?"

"Pink crocodiles."

"What's the code word?" I blurt out suddenly.

The lady looks confused. "I don't know. I'm sorry. I don't know what the code word is. Do you and your dad have a code word? Like in case a stranger approaches you?"

I nod and cough.

"I guess I shouldn't be surprised you don't remember me. I haven't seen you since you were a little girl. I'm Jackie. You used to call me Titi Jack because you couldn't get your mouth around the words Auntie and Jackie."

A distant memory echoes in my head. I do remember something about Titi. I remember stumbling over a long name. I remember a chorus of laughter and my mother picking me up and putting me on her lap.

"Beanstalk," I say quietly. "Your dog. Is she named Beanstalk?"

"That's right." She laughs. "Because she used to jump around like a Mexican jumping bean when she was a puppy. Your mom called her Beanstalk as a joke."

"Jackie and the Beanstalk," I whisper. "I remember. Mom told me stories. I thought it was make-believe. She used to say that's where Tuff came from."

"That's right. My dog, Cassie, had a litter of puppies. Bean's one of them and Tuff's another. You came for a visit when Tuff and Bean were about six months old. They were the last of the litter."

When Aunt Jackie smiles at the memory her eyes sparkle like my mother's and this observation triggers a pang of longing so deep I feel an unexpected urge to run into her arms. But I don't move because I can't, my brain is too busy processing information to divert energy to my legs. Instead I stand anchored in place, swaying like seaweed in an underwater current.

Questions tumble like puppies through my mind. *How could I have an aunt? How did she find me? Why didn't I remember her? Why didn't Dad tell me about her? Why didn't he send me to her instead of making me camp in a ravine alone?* Nothing makes sense and the more I try to piece my past into a cohesive picture, the more elusive the possibilities are.

"It doesn't make sense," I whisper finally.

"I know. You must be very confused. But I promise I am not going to hurt you." She pauses. "Of course, that's exactly what someone who wanted to hurt you would say. Do you want to sit down and talk a bit?"

I nod and sit down on the ground. The lady — Titi Jack or Aunt Jackie or whoever she is — retrieves my sleeping bag from the tent and hands it to me. I wrap it around myself to stop the shivering. Tuff comes to sit down beside me.

The phone vibrates and I check the message.

I'm here. Sup? It's Brandon.

I delete the message and suddenly regret smashing my phone in the library. I so badly want to text Lise and tell her to come back. To hurry! That Tuff is home safe and sound. That maybe we are going to be okay after all.

Aunt Jackie watches me pocket the phone. "Is everything okay?" She asks.

"I want to text Lise, but we only have the one phone."

"Maybe she'll show up soon?" She suggests, then sits down on the ground beside me. I wonder if I should offer her the other sleeping bag to sit on, but she doesn't seem concerned about getting her coat dirty.

"Tell me more about Tuff," I say finally when the silence between us threatens to swallow me whole.

Aunt Jackie perks up. "Well, I remember this one morning we came downstairs and you were curled up with him on the kitchen linoleum, both of you fast asleep. You had your head on his back like a pillow. I took a photo."

"Do you have it still?"

"Yes. But not here."

"Was he happy?"

"To have you sleeping on him? I think so. He looked happy. After that day you refused to go anywhere without him. So your mother flew him home to Florida when you left."

Beanstalk makes her way back to the centre of camp and lies down at Tuff's feet. They pant in unison, their long pink tongues drooping from their mouths.

"Tell me again how you found Tuff? How did you find me here?"

"I don't live far from here. Why don't you come to my place and get warm? I'll make you a bowl of soup and a cup of hot tea and tell you everything."

When I hesitate, she continues. "At least come up and look at the house. If you don't feel safe coming inside, we can go somewhere public and talk. But we should at least go somewhere warm."

"Can Tuff come, too?"

"Of course. Let's go before this snow turns to freezing rain. They're calling for some messy weather this afternoon."

She reaches out her hand and this time I take it. She pulls me to a stand, grabs me in a hug, and holds on as if she's just rescued me from drowning in the cold grey waters of Lake Ontario.

"What about Lise?" I remember suddenly. "She's still out looking for Tuff. We thought he was lost."

Aunt Jackie looks around the campsite. "Lise stays here with you?"

"She normally stays at the shelter, but she didn't want me to be alone." A coughing spasm takes hold of me. When I catch my breath I say, "She thinks I'm too sick."

"She's right. You are too sick. Why don't we leave her a note? When she gets back maybe she can come to my house?"

I pick up the remnants of a cracker box and Aunt Jackie rummages in her purse for a pen. I start to write, then pause.

"Where do you live?"

"Amelia Street. Number nine."

"Wait! I know that house. The stone one with the white fence and yellow door."

"That's it. You remember?"

"No. But we walk by sometimes. Tuff likes to pee on your gatepost."

Aunt Jackie laughs and I write the note.

Lise: Tuff came back safe. He brought my aunt with him. It sounds crazy, but it's no joke. She says to meet us at her house at 9 Amelia Street. You know the place Tuff likes to pee? Please come as soon as you can. Harbour. PS I left your phone in the sleeping bag.

I lay the note inside the flap, zip up the tent, and walk with my aunt up the side of the ravine while Tuff and Bean race ahead.

Walking uphill makes me sweat so I feel hot and cold at the same time. When I shiver, Aunt Jackie reaches over and lays her palm against my cheek, then on my forehead. It reminds me of having the chicken pox when I was little and stuck in bed. Mom felt my forehead every five minutes, or so it seemed at the time, and I remember complaining to her to stop touching me.

"Do you have kids?" I ask between coughs.

"No. It's just me and Bean."

"Do you like kids?"

"Some kids, yes." She pauses, then adds, "I always liked you."

We emerge from the trees and wait for an opening in the traffic before crossing the street. The cars spray slush as they pass and Aunt Jackie pulls me out of the way.

"I was wondering, did we go to Centre Island when I was little? When we visited you?"

Aunt Jackie beams. "Yes! Do you remember?"

"No, but I saw a picture of me by the Ferris wheel. It was on a poster in the subway tunnel."

"I gave that picture to the police. Your mother's in the original, but they cropped her out."

Aunt Jackie is holding both leashes and leans down to untangle Tuff from Bean. It's obvious neither of them is used to walking with a companion. While we're stopped, Bean licks Tuff's face and when Tuff looks back at me, I swear he's smiling.

"How did you find Tuff?" I think I asked already but I can't remember the answer. It's like my brain is overloaded and running on half power at the same time.

"He found me, actually. When I woke up this morning he was waiting by the gate. Bean wouldn't stop barking when she saw him. So I let Tuff into the yard and they started to play. I think he remembers us. Or maybe it's wishful thinking. But he sure was happy to see me and when he came into the yard he went right to the back door where I used to feed him and Bean."

"Tuff had breakfast?"

"A bowl of kibble mixed with half a can of meaty beef."

"I bet he liked that."

Aunt Jackie puts her arm around me and squeezes my shoulder. "I can't believe you're here. With me. Finally."

*   *   *

Aunt Jackie's house is compact by some people's standards but spacious by mine. The entrance is inviting, like the very building is beckoning me to step inside. I stop in the front hall to examine a series of black-framed photos on the wall.

"That's me?" I ask pointing to a picture of a small girl looking lost in a field of tall grass.

"It is. We used to take the dogs down to the ravine every morning for a walk. You picked a fistful of wildflowers for your mom just after that photo was taken."

I stop in front of the next photo. It's a picture of my mother long before I was born. She's sitting on a bench with a younger version of Aunt Jackie.

"How old is she here?"

"She's eighteen and I'm twenty. We took a road trip that summer out to Vancouver. Just the two of us. Our father let us take his car, which was a miracle in itself. We were gone all summer, and so broke we ended up camping in truck stops and parking lots for two weeks."

"Dad met her in Vancouver."

"That's right. They met on the ferry to Vancouver Island."

"He was playing his guitar and singing on the deck. He played 'Brown Eyed Girl.'"

I know these bits of my parents' history from my father retelling them over and over, but it suddenly dawns on me that Aunt Jackie had been with them, that she knows my father, too, that my parents didn't meet and live in a vacuum before I was born.

Aunt Jackie chuckles quietly. "He had a crowd around him listening and singing along. But when he sang that song he never took his eyes off your mother."

"He's dead. I think."

"I know, sweetheart. And I'm sorry."

CHAPTER 16

I STAND IN the shower and watch the dirt stream off my body then disappear down the drain. The water is as hot as I can stand and the heat soaks deep into my bones until it melts the ice lodged there. I lather the soap until my hands are gloved with bubbles, then wash my face and neck and arms over and over until the water runs clear. I would stay in the steamy heaven all day if it were possible, but it isn't. When the water starts to lose its heat, I take a last deep breath of steam. Then I shut off the taps, wrap myself in a large, soft bathrobe, and pad to the bedroom across the hall.

The room is white and clean with soft blue and lime-green accents. The bed is more luxurious than anything I could imagine, with a thick feather duvet and a bank of colourful pillows. Everything smells like laundry detergent and fresh flowers and when I climb between the sheets, I sink into the softness of my very own cloud.

"Lucky for you I made a pot of chicken soup last night."

Aunt Jackie walks into the room carrying a tray and sets it down on the bed stand. She hands me a steaming, oversized mug of soup that smells so delicious I can barely wait for it to cool down. I blow on it briefly, then start tipping it down my throat as fast as I can.

"So good," I mutter between mouthfuls. "Like my mom's."

"It was our grandmother's recipe."

When I finish the first mug, she hands me a plate of buttered toast and heads back to the kitchen for seconds.

"I still don't understand how you found me," I say, when the urgency to fill my stomach has settled.

"Oh, it's not rocket science. I noticed Tuff smelled smoky when he showed up and I remembered the police told me they were trying to locate a girl camped down in the ravine, in case it was you. I put two and two together and went looking. Tuff did the rest."

When I finish the second mug of soup I lean back into the pillows and close my eyes. Already I feel the cold memory of the ravine shrinking away.

"You knew I was in Toronto?"

Aunt Jackie takes the empty mug and sets it on the tray, then perches on the edge of the bed. I shift over to make more room.

"I did after the police came looking for you. Or looking for information about you, maybe that's more accurate."

"I don't understand. How did they know to come here?"

She reaches over and wipes a strand of hair out of my face, a strand that escaped Lise's scissors.

"I filed a missing person's report for you, years ago, when I stopped hearing from your dad and the private detectives I hired couldn't turn up anything about either of you. The police updated me a couple of times since then, just saying they had this piece of information or that. But nothing was ever conclusive. So when they suspected you were in Toronto, they came to me. I gave them the picture and they made the posters."

There are twenty questions jostling for first place in my mind and it's difficult to know which to ask first. "But why did they think to look in Toronto?"

"They said there was only one number in the call history on your dad's phone when they found him and it was yours. When they called it, someone answered and said you were in Toronto."

"Lise! The day she picked up the phone in the library. She must have told them I was in Toronto. But I still don't know how that led them to look in the ravine."

"That's the strange part. Apparently a librarian saw the poster and told them to look for somewhere nearby where a girl could camp. I guess they thought of the ravine."

Erica's face flashes in my mind. How do I explain everything to Aunt Jackie in a way that makes sense — Dad's reading list and needing a library card, conjuring her address, washing in the fifth-floor sink, taking the sleeping bags into the library, and making up a story about camping in Algonquin Park? I try some sentences in my head but none of them seem right and the urgency to talk drifts away like clouds blowing out to sea. I get lost in the thoughts and chase them around inside my head for a few moments too long. In the stillness, sleep catches up and overrides my brain.

*   *   *

The bedroom is dark when I wake up, but enough light seeps in from around the edges of the door that I can make out the shapes of furniture: the pine armoire on the far wall, a dresser to my left, an old steamer trunk under the window. At first I'm confused about where I am and whose voices are coming from down the hall. But then I recognize the light music of Aunt Jackie's laughter, like wind chimes on a summer's day, and the low murmur of a girl with a protective veneer.

I climb out of the big, soft bed and reluctantly leave the warmth behind me. The old plank flooring feels cool against my bare feet as I walk toward the light and laughter. Lise and Aunt Jackie are sitting at the kitchen table, a black photo album open between them. Tuff and Bean are sharing a dog bed in the corner. Tuff thumps his tail when he sees me, but doesn't raise his head. Lise has showered and changed into clothes she must have borrowed from Aunt Jackie because they're loose and long on her petite frame. She's taken the rings out of her eyebrows and I see her for the first time without eyeliner and mascara. She looks younger, sweeter, more vulnerable, and nothing like a kid who's spent two years living on the street and in shelters. I pull the robe around myself and cover a cough with my elbow. They turn in unison to greet me.

"Harbour! Hello. You're awake." Aunt Jackie rises and pulls out a chair. I scurry forward and sit with my right ankle tucked under my left leg.

"Have I been sleeping long?"

"A couple of hours. How're you feeling?"

"Better, I think." I swallow and wince. "My throat hurts."

Aunt Jackie gets up and bustles around the kitchen. She fills the kettle, cuts lemon, scoops honey, and peels fresh ginger. Her movements are precise and efficient. Lise and I look at each other across the table. It feels awkward to have something between us and to be sitting in a warm, clean kitchen with a stranger who is my aunt.

"You got my note?"

She nods.

"I've offered Lise a bed for the night. I assume you don't mind?" Aunt Jackie says over her shoulder.

Lise pulls a face and I cough. "No. I don't mind. Of course not. Thanks."

Aunt Jackie brings me a steaming mug wrapped in a napkin.

"This will make it feel better, I promise. But it's very hot so be careful. Lise, would you like a refill?"

"I'm too stuffed," Lise says and rubs her tummy. "Even for another cup of tea. It was delicious, though." She looks more comfortable than I've seen her in a long time.

I sip the sweet gingery tea and the heat burns down my throat.

"Check this out." Lise pushes the photo book toward me. She points at a picture and I have to look close to recognize myself sitting with Tuff on the front steps of a stone house. My legs are short and pudgy and my cheeks round and fat, but my hair is the same wild mane as my mother's and aunt's. Tuff, the puppy, is half sitting on my lap, licking my chin, and I'm laughing. In my outstretched hand is a soggy ice cream cone.

"That's here?"

Aunt Jackie nods.

"Look how cute Tuff is," I say.

"Look how cute you are," Aunt Jackie counters.

There are other photos of me and Mom and Dad: eating candy floss at the amusement park with the log flume ride in the background; building a sand castle on a beach; walking through a park with Tuff, who is holding a stick in his mouth. In one photo Dad is carrying me on his shoulders, in another Mom is sitting in his lap and the two of them are beaming at the camera. There's a picture of Dad playing his ukulele on one end of a couch and Mom watching him from the other end, a dreamy look on her face. All of the photos are secured by their corners with little black triangles and underneath there are captions written in silver ink.

"How old was I?"

"Four."

"Did we visit a lot?"

"Not after that time. But you were up one time before. You and your mother came when you were a baby, about ten months old."

I flip through the photo album and examine every detail of every picture. Eventually Lise yawns.

"I think I need to show Lise to her room."

I look up at Lise and she smiles. It's a short, tentative smile, but it suits her.

"You don't mind spending the night?" I ask.

"Are you kidding? Did you see the bed? There're more pillows on one bed in this house than in the entire shelter."

Lise follows Aunt Jackie down the hall and as she leaves the kitchen she turns back and waves good night. I raise my hand briefly before she disappears. When I'm alone I look around. The kitchen is clean and orderly with stainless-steel counters and bright yellow accents. From where I'm sitting I can see a mud room, the back door, and rows of coat hooks attached to the wall. There are various jackets hung up, including the long black coat Aunt Jackie wore down to the ravine, as well as a variety of hats and scarves.

When Aunt Jackie returns she makes me a fresh cup of ginger tea and we sit at the table to talk.

"There's something I don't understand," I say in a low voice.

"What's that?"

"You said Dad only had one number on his phone?"

"That's what the police said. The call history showed he only ever called the one number."

"But I used to hear him talking on it all the time, after I went to bed. Sometimes he'd talk for hours."

Aunt Jackie shrugs. "I don't know what to say. They told me yours was the only number ever called on his phone. Maybe it was a different phone. Maybe he got a new one after you left?"

I shake my head. "Maybe. But I don't think so."

"Why not?"

"Because Dad didn't go on land. Not for the last few years, at least. He didn't trust people much. I ran all the errands. So once I left, he had no way to get a new phone. That probably sounds strange to you."

"Not really, not knowing your dad the way I do."

I look down at the photo album and flip pages back and forth. I'm not really looking at the photos, but I'm afraid to look up because I can feel Aunt Jackie studying me. I can feel that she has something more to say and I'm reluctant to hear what it is.

"Did you know he was sick?" She stops herself and searches for words on the ceiling.

"Sick? From what?" I ask, although I am not entirely surprised to hear a confession surfacing.

"A mental illness. Schizophrenia."

Of all the things I expected to hear, this wasn't it. And yet I'm not shocked or outraged by her statement.

"Dad? Are you sure?"

"He was diagnosed a couple of years after he met your mom, before you were born. She always made sure he took his meds. I think she kept him grounded. After she died, though, he came unhinged a bit. It was so terrible, so traumatic what happened that night. I think something snapped. He'd call up and ramble about all kinds of things. I could barely follow his train of thought sometimes. Other times he would say the most startlingly beautiful things about life, about being a father, about how much he loved your mother."

A thought that has been trying to scratch to the surface of my mind breaks through suddenly and I can't avoid it no matter how much I want to will it out of existence.

"Lately I've been wondering something. There's so much I don't know and don't understand. Do you think it's possible that he killed her? Like by accident, maybe?"

"No. Absolutely not. He was never even a suspect. The police found evidence linking the bullets found in your house to other home invasions in the area. And there were fingerprints and DNA. There was definitely an intruder."

"They never caught him?"

"Not yet."

"Dad took me that night. I heard the shots, and then Dad took me away on the boat, so I didn't know. I mean, lately I've started to wonder what really happened."

"You were so young. It's possible you've mixed up two nights. Memory is strange that way. He did take you aboard to live shortly after. He took you down to Mexico and all around the Caribbean. It was something he and your mom had been planning for the family. I think your mother would be happy to know he did that with you. And being on the boat seemed to help. He seemed more settled when you lived aboard."

"Was there a funeral?"

"There was. I came down and stayed a couple of weeks afterwards. I tried to help him get sorted. He didn't want to go to anyone in his family. He didn't trust them, even then, except for one stepbrother. He was so distraught, but it was understandable, right?"

I try to remember Aunt Jackie in our house on Pelican Way. But my mind lines up the few predictable memories I have of living in that house and stops. I can't seem to squeeze any new memories from my brain.

"Your father said he was afraid of being in the house after that, and I think staying in one place made him nervous. He always talked like someone was after him, but the police were convinced it was a random event, that it was a robbery gone wrong."

I take the last sip of the gingery tea. It's still sweet, but the heat has disappeared. I cough and feel a heavy exhaustion weighing me down. Aunt Jackie crosses the kitchen and comes back with a brown bottle and a tablespoon.

"I've made you a doctor's appointment for the morning, but in the meantime I'm going to give you some cough syrup and send you to bed."

"I hate cough syrup."

She pours bright red liquid onto the spoon and stands in front of me. "Everybody does. Open up."

The syrup is sweet and bitter at the same time and catches in the back of my throat. I gag and sputter.

"Oh, come on. It wasn't that bad."

She returns the bottle to the cupboard and puts the spoon in the sink with a clink. Then she ushers me from the kitchen.

I rub the bristly hairs on the back of my head as we walk.

"I was thinking, when I'm feeling better, I need to get a haircut. Lise didn't do a very good job on this one."

CHAPTER 17

I WATCH ERICA from across the lobby of the library. She's behind the information desk, standing in front of a computer terminal and talking to a middle-aged man in an expensive-looking winter jacket. She smiles at him, checks the computer once more, then pulls at the bottom of her cardigan before delivering some final news. I'm too far away to hear what they're talking about, but this is how I imagine their exchange:

"I'm sorry. That book is checked out. It's been out since summer, actually."

"Out since summer! Some people have no manners. Do they think this is their private collection?"

"I'm so sorry. I'd call with a reminder that it's overdue but there's no number on file for this patron."

"No number on file! That's ridiculous. That shouldn't be allowed. You should revisit your lending policies and only lend books to responsible adults."

"I do apologize, again. I'll call you as soon as it comes back in."

Erica delivers her final line sweetly, trying her best to prevent a full-blown escalation. But the man doesn't end the conversation politely just because Erica has displayed impeccable manners, and she adjusts her reading glasses nervously. He mutters and harrumphs under his breath before zipping up his jacket and heading toward the glass doors.

Or maybe that isn't how their conversation goes at all, but it's what my guilty mind scripts just the same.

I shift the pack on my back and approach the counter. Erica glances up when she sees me standing in front of her, then does one of those double-take kind of looks where you can't believe what you're seeing is really there.

"Harbour," she says brightly, but with a hint of a question. Her eyes scan my face and travel down to my waist. I know how different I look from the last time she saw me.

"You got your hair cut."

I step forward until I can feel the hard counter press against my body. At the same time I put my hand to the back of my head. I'm still not used to short hair.

"Yeah. A couple of weeks ago. It's already grown in a bit."

"It looks very stylish."

"Thanks. It wasn't intentional, at first."

The air is charged with an awkward silence and I worry she's not going to say anything else. But then she takes a deep breath.

"I haven't seen you in ages. Do you have Tuff with you?"

Of course she remembered to ask about Tuff, I think. So much has happened to me since I last saw her, it feels as though I have a million things to share. But to her, I'm just another regular passing through the lobby.

"I left him home today. It's not very nice out."

Together we glance out the glass doors at the grey day and blowing snow.

"But he's well?"

"Yeah, he's great."

This time I rush to fill the gap in our conversation before it turns awkward. "I brought you something."

I swing my backpack onto the counter and rummage in the front pocket. After a moment I pull out an envelope and hand it to her. She examines it longer than I expect her to, which makes me squirm. I shift from one leg to another.

"It's a piece of mail," I prompt finally. "With my name and address on it. And the postal code, which you'll be happy to know I've finally committed to memory."

The expression on Erica's face is hard to decipher when she looks up. Is she happy, or suspicious? She blinks like maybe her eyes are playing tricks on her. But she doesn't speak.

"I'm surprised, too," I suggest, not knowing what else to say, or how much. I'm sure a thousand questions are brawling inside her head.

She studies me for a moment before saying, "So we can get you a permanent card!"

"Yes, at last." I want to apologize for the delay, and thank her for always being so kind to me, but something keeps me from stumbling headlong into a tricky explanation.

Erica turns to the computer and begins to type. She uses the mouse to click several boxes, then types some more, using the envelope as a guide.

"I have something else for you," I say, reaching into my backpack again.

I hand her Paramahansa Yogananda's translation of *The Bhagavad Gita*.

"It's a new copy. The other one got damaged. I'm sorry."

Erica takes the book and places it on the counter. Her hand lingers on it protectively, as if there's something sacred about it, or in it.

"Thanks for replacing it. It will take us a week or so to get it into circulation, but there's a hold on it. So your timing is great."

"Someone else wants to read Yogananda?"

"Yes. Me, actually." She blushes slightly.

"Did you read his autobiography?"

"I did. And I enjoyed it very much, thanks to you and your dad."

I smile to myself when I think about the repercussions of Dad's reading list, how his influence is rippling out into the world even though he's no longer in it. I think about how even the smallest of his ideas might go on forever like a wave that travels across an entire ocean before bouncing off a rocky shore. The thought brings me comfort and I remind myself to visit it again later, perhaps as I lie in the dark waiting for sleep to come.

"How is your reading list coming along?" Erica asks before walking to the far end of the counter. She returns with an apology for interrupting our conversation.

"Actually, I've given it up."

Her face falls and I feel a surge of alarm when her expression changes.

"Don't worry. I'm still doing lots of reading — for school."

Erica's face brightens. "You're in school!"

"I'm going to an alternative learning centre. I didn't think I'd fit into a regular high school. Too much structure. Too many rules. Just not me."

"Do you like it?"

"I do. I'm taking a course in religious studies. Right now we're on Islam. It's fascinating."

"You'll certainly have a head start when you get to Hinduism." Erica's voice is light and musical when she says this, so melodic that I don't want the sound to ever end.

"I'm taking English, too. We just finished *1984*."

"So you *do* have plenty of reading to keep you busy."

I nod. "I'll never stop reading."

"I hope that means I'll still get to see plenty of you," she says and hands me a plastic card the size of my old credit card.

"Definitely," I say. "You have a great section on world religions."

I tuck the card into the front pocket of my backpack, zip it up and turn to go. My next destination is the shelter.

"It was good seeing you again, Erica."

"You too. Stay warm."

I've taken a few steps across the lobby when she calls out, "Don't lose that card."

I glance over my shoulder to flash her a smile and in that moment catch a look of happy wonder dart across her face, a look as fleeting as a fish moving among the shadows of a sunlit reef.

*   *   *

Seeing Lise is still a highlight of my day, and I approach the shelter with a warm sense of anticipation. Joyce pops her head through the door of her office when she hears me walk inside. It's the end of the day, so a busy time. Some people are coming back after a long cold afternoon and others are popping outside for a cigarette. The door groans open behind me and I feel a cool draft on the back of my legs.

"Harbour Mandrayke," Joyce says energetically when she sees me. "What a nice surprise."

I'm always amazed by how welcome Joyce can make a person feel with so few words.

"Is Lise here?" I ask and step farther inside so people can get past me.

"She is. She got back a few minutes ago."

I pull off my winter hat and shove it in my pocket, then undo my jacket so I don't overheat on my way up the stairs.

"Is it okay if I go up?"

Joyce nods and shields her eyes before stepping back into her office. Technically non-residents aren't supposed to wander around the shelter, but Joyce has a way of turning a blind eye where Lise is concerned. Apparently I fall into the "see no evil" category.

The door to Lise's room is slightly ajar. I knock lightly and walk in at the same time. Lise looks up from where she's sitting on her bed and closes a Smart Serve workbook over her fingers. I peel off my jacket and park my butt on the bed across from her.

"How'd it go today?"

She sighs. "I think it went okay. For someone like you, it'd be a no-brainer. But school was never my thing."

She no longer has long, dark dreadlocks framing her face. Instead she has short hair, like mine. She teases that we look like a couple of dudes, but I think she looks prettier, and more mainstream, without them. She's also lightened up her eye makeup and left the rings out of her eyebrow. She looks like she could be a model for H&M or Forever 21, or something.

"Still, you think you passed?"

"I have to get an eighty. So I dunno."

"What if you don't pass?"

"I can take the test again."

"I'm sure you passed, but if you didn't, I can help you study before you do it again."

"Thanks," she says. She tosses the workbook onto the end of her bed. "How was your day at brainiac school?"

"It's not brainiac school," I protest. "It's just a regular school with fewer rules."

Lise and I have had the same conversation at least ten times in the past week.

"Oh, come on. You know you're one of those intellectual elites."

I laugh. "Nice try. My entire education has been based on the whims of my father. So while I might know a lot about the engine of a Porsche 911, I have no knowledge of art history."

"At least you know art history is a thing," she points out stubbornly.

I pick up a pen off the table between the beds and throw it at her.

"You have to get over your victim complex," I say, smiling.

"You have to get over *yourself*," she teases, lobbing the pen back at me.

I duck so that the pen hits the wall. Then, to humour her, I spill some details about my day. "I have an essay to write by next week. Like a thousand words. I've never written an essay before. But the teacher spent a bit of time with me today explaining what I need to do."

"You don't know how good you had it, not having to write essays before."

"To be honest, I kinda always wanted to go to school. I'm looking forward to this."

Lise rolls her eyes but doesn't say anything sarcastic, so I continue.

"And anyway, you're the one always dissing my dad for not being a good parent."

The tone in the room shifts. Suddenly the ceiling seems higher, the temperature cooler. Lise looks down at her lap, then back at me.

"I'm sorry for all the bad things I said about him. I didn't mean any of them. I'm sure he was a great guy. Like, he made you and you're all right. So how bad could he have been? Right?" She pauses, then adds in a quieter voice, "I'm sorry I won't get to meet him."

"No more cooking in the galley," I say brightly, trying to lighten the mood.

"No more peeing in the head," she counters.

I smile sadly. "So much for our plans to go out to Toronto Island on *Starlight*."

"That's okay. We'll make new plans. Like with Aunt Jackie. But I think I would have liked him."

"You would have. Definitely. Especially on his good days. The other days, well, he was hard to handle sometimes."

Lise raises her eyebrows. It's an exaggerated expression meant to signal her surprise. "Talk about progress. Your counsellor would be proud. You've never admitted that before. At least not to me."

"It's strange. Sometimes I wake up in the middle of the night with my heart racing, panicking because I've remembered for, like, the thousandth time that I'm never going to see him again. And every day when I wake up I have to readjust to the fact that he had a mental illness, that there was no plan to blow up the world stored in a microchip under Tuff's skin. It's like every day I'm a bit more deprogrammed. But that makes me sad, too. Like, will I ever know what was real and what wasn't? It makes me question everything I've ever known. Sometimes it sinks me. I feel like I'm in the ocean holding on to a hundred-pound ball of lead. But sometimes I don't care at all. When I boil it all down, he was still him. I loved him, despite some chemical misfire in his brain."

"He must have loved you, too, to be able to send you up here alone. Especially when he knew how much he needed you."

"Exactly. He had a strange way of showing it sometimes, but being my dad was the most important thing to him."

Lise lies back and studies the ceiling. "You know, you're kind of lucky. I mean, not completely lucky, obviously. But some kids never have anyone who cares that much. I mean, I didn't have anyone — like an adult — until I met Joyce."

"I definitely have stuff to be thankful for," I murmur. "I couldn't have imagined saying that two weeks ago, but things can change so fast. In a single instant. A flash."

The echo of footfalls and subdued greetings fill the hallway as people head to the showers or to the kitchen for dinner. I see their shadows flash across the doorway, but I don't look up to see who it is. The mood in Lise's room contrasts most of the other rooms in the shelter. Lise and I are happy, and together we're making plans for our futures.

"I should go. If you don't shower soon you'll miss the hot water. And Aunt Jackie will be expecting me."

Lise sits up and swings her legs onto the floor in one fluid motion. "See ya tomorrow?"

"You know it. Text me your test results when you get them."

"Let me know if you need any help with your essay." Lise laughs.

＊　　　＊　　　＊

By the time I hit the street again, the temperature has dropped and the night sky has unfolded its dark cloak over the city. Over and over I'm startled by how early darkness arrives in winter and how much colder it feels at night. I pull up my hood and tuck my face into my scarf. The snow is falling fast and turning the overhead streetlights into shimmering yellow orbs. It's a mesmerizing illusion that I stop and watch even though it means people have to step around me on the sidewalk. Understanding at last how cold winter really can get in Canada, I refuse to let myself play the "what if" game and instead focus on "what is."

I kick through the snow on my way to Cabbagetown. Now that I have a warm bed every night, I've discovered something magical about a new snowfall. I've noticed how a thick blanket of snow muffles the harsh sounds of the city and covers the imperfections until everything feels close and safe. Perhaps my childhood fantasy to build a snowman and go tobogganing wasn't foolish after all.

It's not a long walk from the shelter, but long enough that a flush of happiness washes over me when I turn onto Amelia Street. I open the white picket gate and step through. The house is glowing with yellow light. It spills out of every window and brightens the snow in the front yard. Music comes from inside and I stop for a moment to watch Aunt Jackie through the window. She's curled up on the couch with Tuff and Bean, reading a book and sipping a mug of what I expect is ginger tea. *That's my family*, I think. *This is the home Dad sent me to find.*

CHAPTER 18

FROM ABOVE, MIAMI looks surreal. It looks like a toy. A circuit board. I know the geography of the waterways the way I knew the veins on Dad's hands or the wrinkles around his eyes when he squinted into the sun. I know what it's like to pull up alongside the immense cruise ships and feel like a speck of dirt floating on the water, and yet, from above, through the small square window against which I am pressing my forehead, the same ships look like decorations on a cake. It's hard to reconcile the two realities and merge them into one truth. Is it a massive hunk of metal and material excess or a tiny piece of a board game?

Hit and sunk.

"He's really dead," I mutter half to myself and half to the world at large. Even though I've known for weeks, somehow this trip to Miami is making it real.

Aunt Jackie reaches over and squeezes my hand.

"*Starlight* was my whole world once. Now she's like one of those tiny pieces of debris floating on the water down there."

"From down there we're just a speck, too. A speck in the sky."

Aunt Jackie's reminder has a strange effect. It makes my world flip upside down. I think of all the times I stretched out on the bow of *Starlight* and watched planes fly overhead. I spent hours tracking jets across the blue sky. As a small child, I wondered what it would be like to be in one, what I would be able to see, if I'd be afraid of the height or of falling out of the plane and tumbling to the ground. And now I've reversed roles. I'm looking down. I'm among the clouds for the first time in my life, staring down at my father's grave.

"I'm afraid to see *Starlight*," I admit finally, though I'm sure it's not much of a revelation to Aunt Jackie. "I'm afraid to see what happened to her."

"Let's not think about it today. Tonight we'll get to our room and relax. Tomorrow we can take as it comes."

I love the way Aunt Jackie breaks big problems into small chunks. She orders the world in a way that makes it seem safe and manageable. Dad didn't do that. If anything, his approach fragmented the world, took big pieces and created smaller and smaller shards that never quite fit back together to make anything whole. I didn't see that at the time, but I do now. Every day another gear fits into place and a new part of the machine turns.

A stewardess rolls the drink cart up to our seats and locks the wheels. She hands each of us a package of snack crackers and offers us a drink. Aunt Jackie orders a Coke and I order an orange juice.

"Should I be nervous about meeting my step-uncle?"

"Not at all. He's a great guy. I met him a few times when I was down visiting your mom."

"I found him hard to talk to. Maybe it was the shock of hearing me on the other end of the phone after so many years. How did he sound to you?"

"Surprised. Relieved. And maybe a little bit guilty, too, I think, that he didn't do more to find you. He's worried about how you coped alone with your dad all those years."

"Dad took good care of me," I say a little defensively, then pause to consider the truth of this statement. I sip my juice. "There were some weird things, sometimes, I guess. But mostly I had an amazing childhood."

Aunt Jackie smirks at me and shakes her head.

"What?"

"Nothing. It's just that you talk like you're an adult when you're only fourteen. You have lots of childhood left."

I can't help but smile back and hope she's right, but part of me knows I haven't been a child in years. And I'm okay with that.

Aunt Jackie leans forward and rummages in her purse. When she sits back up, she hands me a small rectangular parcel.

"What's this for?" I ask suspiciously.

"I dunno," she laughs. "Does it have to be for something? Can't I just get you a present?"

I look at the present in my lap and then at her.

"Just open it already," she says and bumps her shoulder against mine. "You're worse than Tuff Stuff. Suspicious of everything."

"I wish Tuff was here. He won't get to say goodbye. *Starlight* was his home, too."

"I know. It feels wrong not to have him along. But he's in good hands at home with Lise. And Bean won't let him mope around for even a second."

"It's going to be a long week. But I know I'll be glad I did it in the long run. You know, for closure."

"You made a brave decision coming down. But I'm glad you did. We'll both get some closure. And then we can start fresh." Her voice weakens, catches. It sounds like she's going to cry. Then she clears her throat. "Would you just open that present? Please?"

The box is wrapped in blue paper with white clouds and tied with a navy-blue ribbon. It's almost too pretty to open, but I slowly untie the ribbon and unwrap the paper. Inside is a new iPhone, the latest model, already protected by a LifeProof case.

"I wasn't expecting a present. But thank you. For this and for coming down with me. For *everything*." Now it's my turn for my voice to catch on the tears pooling in the back of my throat.

I lean over in my seat and give her a tight, awkward hug.

"Just so you know," Aunt Jackie says, tapping the phone in my hand, "it's charged."

I haven't had a phone since I smashed mine in the library, but I haven't much missed it either. Without Dad I haven't needed one. I mean, I only really know Lise and Aunt Jackie and I've seen them both every day. As I power up the phone, future Harbour flashes through my mind and I see my contact list with dozens of names. I see an inbox full of messages from friends — school friends and work friends and maybe even Erica.

"It's not really about the phone. It's more about what's *in* the phone," Aunt Jackie says as she opens her packet of snack crackers and sips her Coke.

I flip through the icons while my brain tries to puzzle together the meaning of the phone in my hands. What's *in* the phone, I wonder? I look up the contacts and see she's inputted hers and Lise's numbers. I see she's set the ringtone and test it only to discover it's a recording of Tuff and Bean barking. I go to the photos and see pictures of Lise and Tuff, Jackie and Bean, and then the dogs romping through the park. There's even a photo of Aunt Jackie's house on Amelia Street.

"Thanks," I say again, with more sincerity.

"Try the videos," she suggests.

I scroll to the video icon and my breath catches deep inside my chest when I see a file called "E.D. Mandrayke's Ukulele Serenades." I look at Aunt Jackie to be sure there's no mistake.

"Lise saved your memory card. They're all there."

I open the folder to be sure she's telling the truth. And although all the videos I ever recorded of Dad are there, listed alphabetically by song name, I'm still afraid there's going to be a glitch that ends in disappointment. My hands tremble worse than my voice.

"Do you want to see one?"

"Of course. I loved your dad's singing. He was so talented."

I pick "Here Comes the Sun" and watch with a pounding heart while Dad shows up on screen, crunched into as small a space as he can manage with his ukulele. Seeing his face is like having a fifty-pound weight lifted off my chest. When he finishes the song and the screen fills with a beautiful cloud-streaked sunset, I can barely find the words to say thank you again.

"I didn't think I'd ever see these again. This is the best present ever. Ever."

"Lise is the one to thank for rescuing your memory card."

"She's the best friend ever. Ever. EVER."

Aunt Jackie smiles, almost sadly, then turns her head to look down the aisle. While she's turned away I wipe a tear from my eye and try to decipher the expression I just witnessed. Was she sad for me? Or for Dad? Or maybe for Mom?

"Do you think Dad sent me to you in some round-about way?" I ask when she's facing forward again and leaning back in her seat.

"I do. Somehow through all the confusion in his world, he kept you safe."

*   *   *

My step-uncle's house backs onto the Intracoastal near Jupiter, and I know exactly where we are before we've even climbed out of the rental car. I scan the neighbour-hood and wonder if my long-ago playmate still lives next door. I wonder if he remembers me.

Aunt Jackie comes around to the passenger side of the car and opens my door at the same time as a tall man steps out the front door. He's wearing cargo shorts and a golf shirt, and he has short, grey hair. There's an awkward moment in the driveway while we decide what introductions need to be made. Finally Aunt Jackie steps forward with a hug.

"Dennis! You're looking well. I'm sure Harbour has changed quite a bit since you last saw her."

My step-uncle smiles warmly, turning from Aunt Jackie to me and back. "It's great to see you — *both* — again."

The sun is hot on my shoulders and I feel the faint tickle between my shoulder blades as a droplet of sweat rolls down my back. Six months in Canada and already I've lost my tolerance for the Florida sun. My father was a pure southern boy. He never could have survived the Canadian cold.

"Please, come inside for a cold drink," Dennis says as he gestures to the front door.

I step forward and lead Aunt Jackie into this house I've only ever known from the outside looking in. Cool air envelopes us and I shiver slightly as the sweat at my temples meets the air conditioning. We kick off our sandals in the foyer, then follow him through to the kitchen where a bank of windows reveals an impressive view over the pool and dock, and, beyond, the Intracoastal Waterway.

"You have a beautiful house," Aunt Jackie says as she accepts a tall glass filled with ice and lemonade.

My step-uncle acknowledges the comment graciously, but in a way that makes me know he's heard it plenty of times before.

I glance around the house and it *is* beautiful. It looks like a picture from a home decorating magazine, with a

Southern Florida kind of vibe. There's bamboo furniture with floral cushions, shell-filled glass lamps, a seagrass carpet, and a banana leaf plant in the corner.

"Please sit down," Dennis says as he motions toward the family room. I take an armchair by the window and study the view. He and Aunt Jackie sit on a couch across a glass coffee table from me and exchange a few comments about our trip before turning the conversation back to me.

"You've really grown up since I last saw you, Harbour."

My mind scrambles for something appropriate to say, but I get caught trying to decide how I'm expected to address him, this man who obviously has clear memories of me even though I know him only through stories told by my father.

Uncle Dennis? Step-uncle Dennis? Dennis? Mr. Whatsyourlastnameanyway?

He's undaunted by my silence. "Last time I saw you, you were maybe five or six. It was before your mother passed away. You look so much like her."

Passed away makes my mother's death sound infuriatingly passive, but I know he's just trying to be polite by not using the word *murdered*.

I sip my lemonade, then clear my throat. "When did you last talk to my dad?"

Dennis leans back and crosses one leg over the other. He stretches an arm across the back of the couch toward Aunt Jackie.

"Oh, it was over a year ago now. He called to say you were going to sail to Canada and spend some time with your Aunt Jackie. At first I thought it was a, well, ridiculous plan, sailing all that way. But then I thought maybe it was a blessing in disguise. I'm sure a break from that boat would have done you both a world of good. And I could never get him to come here, no matter how many times I invited him."

My mind travels back to the month we spent tied to his dock, swimming in his pool, using his deck furniture. Is it possible he never knew about the time we spent here?

"Did you talk to him often?" I finally manage to ask.

"Not too often. Maybe a couple of times a year. He'd call me out of the blue and leave a number that would work once or twice, then it'd be out of service when I tried it the next time."

"He wasn't very good about keeping track of his phone," I offer.

"You're right there. I think he spent half his income replacing phones and fixing *Starlight*."

I must look confused because Aunt Jackie rushes to fill the awkward silence.

"Dennis has been managing your father's finances since you moved onto *Starlight*."

I look at Dennis and size him up. For some reason my father trusted this man, so I probably should, too.

"I was the executor of his will, too. Did you know?"

I shake my head.

"Of course he left everything to you. And so he should have. But I tell you, I was relieved when your aunt contacted me. There were so many loose ends I couldn't tie up. Until now."

"He left me *Starlight*?" I ask.

"Yes. Although she's suffered some serious damage. But he also left you the house on Pelican Way and his share of the radio stations."

"We still own the house?"

"Yes. There's been a family renting it since you moved out. Your father never mentioned this?"

The glass of lemonade feels heavy in my hand so I put it on the coffee table in front of me. Then I wipe the condensation onto my shorts.

"He didn't like to talk about those days, from when we lived in Stuart."

"The rent money goes into a trust fund for you."

"Would you like to go see it?" Aunt Jackie asks me.

I shake my head. The house on Pelican Way feels like another life, like someone else's life, and it's not someone I want to revisit. I have what I can remember of my mother tucked safely in my head and that's all I need.

"I just want to see *Starlight*."

✳   ✳   ✳

At first glance *Starlight* looks pretty much the same as she always did. Her mast is broken and there's a nasty crack in the hull by the forward deck, but otherwise she's still *Starlight*, still strong and proud, and inviting me to climb aboard. But as I get closer I'm unnerved by her sitting, raised, on metal jacks. Hidden behind the leaves of an overhanging live oak tree, the sun casts a green hue on her white deck. She lies still, drained, motionless without the sea to animate her. I've never seen her out of water and it makes me sad, the way it's sad to see an elephant doing tricks at a circus.

I walk around her slowly. Dad hadn't kept up with the barnacles and now they cling stubbornly to the propeller and keel. He always said the hull of a boat had a story to tell and I look at our story now, at nine years of adventure and mishap. Each patch tells of a time ashore that for me meant new friends and freedom. There are also the inevitable nicks and scrapes in the hull — some that I recognize and some that I know are new, chapters of the story that were written after I left.

I hear the coast guard captain talking, outlining the details of their search-and-rescue mission: how the report came in, how they located her, how they towed her back to port. He talks mostly to Aunt Jackie, but directs certain comments my way, as if my reaction will help him piece together the clues into a finished puzzle.

"She was still floating, partly submerged, when we located her. She had a broken mast."

I listen but I don't react. Instead I run my hand along her hull like I'm comforting a stranded whale.

"She'd been drifting for a couple of weeks. That's just an estimate, of course, based on her condition and that of the deceased, as well as some accounts from other sailors. It could have been longer. There was no sign of any distress signal having been made."

The *deceased*, I think. Dad has been reduced to one impersonal word.

"Where was my father?" I ask, looking back to where the captain and Aunt Jackie are standing near the stern.

Aunt Jackie recoils slightly from my question, but she doesn't stop the captain from answering.

He speaks without apology and this brings me comfort. "He was below, in the forward cabin. It was still dry."

The forward cabin. My cabin. The last dry place. I find it odd that he should include this last observation, as if his being dry makes my father's death easier to accept.

Despite the message he has to deliver, the captain's voice is kind and soothing. I can only imagine how he might have dreaded my arrival. Nobody, not even a professional coast guard captain, wants to tell a kid how her father spent possibly weeks adrift, unnoticed, dead.

No matter how I try to figure it out, I can't come up with a scenario that would account for how Dad — and *Starlight* — ended up that way.

"He must have got caught up in some bad weather, maybe the tail end of that hurricane. Winds that strong could snap a mast. If he was stranded in weather like that …"

The captain's voice drifts off and I look to see what interrupted him. But he has just lost the end of his sentence or thought. He looks down at his feet, then up at the sky as if in prayer. His uniform speaks of authority, which I find calming, although Dad would resist being impressed if he were here. He was a rebel at heart.

I don't contradict the captain, but I know it's impossible that Dad got caught in a storm. Dad started sailing with his father when he was just three years old. And my grandfather started sailing with *his* father at birth. Dad knew too much about sailing to get into trouble. He knew the sea, he had sailing in his blood and, above all else, he respected the weather. There are many unanswered questions, questions I will have to live with the rest of my life. But there is no question in my mind about Dad making a mistake on a sailboat. Something happened to Dad down below, inside *Starlight*, and the mast broke after he was already dead. And what did it really matter what happened? The end of the story is the same and I know I can live with uncertainty.

The captain offers me a hand when I start to climb up onto *Starlight*, but I scramble past him and survey the cockpit. It's scattered with debris and tangled ropes. I take a deep breath and steady myself for what I'll find inside.

Although the hatches are open, everything inside *Starlight* smells like rot and I have to cover my nose to keep from gagging.

"Are you okay in there?" Aunt Jackie calls from below on the ground.

"Fine," I call back. I need to be in *Starlight* alone, just for a few minutes, no matter what I find.

The aft cabin is a mess. It's scattered with scraps of paper and cardboard that have incoherent notes written in Dad's shorthand. There are several maps of the United States, unfolded, crossed with lines and arrows. There are dates, calculations, and random numbers etched in the empty spaces. What puzzles me most are the bits and pieces of debris he must have found floating in the ocean over the past few months: a faded life ring, a plastic milk jug, a cracked buoy, numerous hunks of driftwood with pieces of rope tied to them. I scour the cabin for something that acknowledges me or Tuff, but there's nothing to indicate we were part of his plan, sane or deluded, or that we were even on his mind.

In the galley there are empty tuna and soup tins and crumpled sleeves of crackers. It doesn't look like he restocked from when I left him in July. *July*, I think to myself. It's only been six months since I left Florida and yet everything has changed.

I'll never forget the day I saw Dad for the last time and let it play in my memory, just a few frames in case I remember something I should have noticed, a warning or a sign.

"Four, five weeks tops," he'd said to me on our last afternoon. "Unless there's a low-pressure system on the east coast. It'll go by so fast you'll hardly notice we're apart."

I nodded and forced myself not to cry.

"I'll meet you down at Ashbridges Bay," he said for the thousandth time. Then he pointed to the map on my phone, exactly where he was going to arrive and see me again.

"Right?"

"Right."

"Got it?"

"Got it."

"Any questions?"

"Nope. I got it all here on my phone."

"And your reading list?"

"Right here on my phone, too."

"No slacking off just because I'm not there to remind you."

"No slacking off. I promise."

He manoeuvred the boat until we were hovering just inches from the pier.

"Ready to jump?"

"Ready."

"Tuff, come say goodbye, then go with Harbour."

He hugged Tuff and gave his ears a good scratch. "You take good care of my girl."

I didn't resist or hesitate. I couldn't. He'd been planning and rehearsing every detail with me for months. Tuff and I jumped onto the pier at Bayside Marketplace. It was so intricately planned, I even knew where to buy my lunch that first day and which city bus would take me to the Greyhound terminal.

"Call me from the bus terminal," he called out before he put *Starlight* into reverse and pulled away from the pier.

"I will," I called back and hoisted my backpack onto my shoulders.

The only instruction I disobeyed was that when he dropped us on land, I didn't turn and leave immediately. Instead, I watched him motor away, his back first, then *Starlight*, shrinking in the distance as he headed out toward Key Biscayne. I watched until he vanished in the glinting water and then I watched a bit longer to be sure I wasn't still seeing him. It had been a brilliantly sunny day without a cloud in the sky. We hadn't been able to see Mom's face that morning. Maybe that had been the sign. Maybe it wasn't an *all-clear* signal after all.

My head hurts thinking back and seeing what I couldn't see then. My heart feels tattered. Why did I leave?

I let the memory fade and bring the present into focus again. The forward cabin is the only place not crammed with junk. It looks the same as it did when I left. The sides of the hull are still covered with my artwork and old photos of Dad and Mom and me. My clothes are still piled in the drawers, my polka-dot bedding is still on the mattress. He must have been sleeping here because it was the only uncluttered surface left. In fact, the only sign Dad was using the space at all is his Miami Dolphins water bottle and his ukulele, which is tucked into the cubby above my bunk. I pick up the ukulele and turn to leave. Then I stop and take down all of the photos and my artwork, and I tuck them into the ukulele case.

It's a relief to breathe the fresh Florida air when I climb back on deck. It smells of the ocean and my childhood. It smells of my past.

"Are you okay?" Aunt Jackie says. She's looking up at me, her hand clasping the brim of her bright yellow sun hat.

I reach down and hand her the ukulele case.

"I am. I really am," I say, and climb down the ladder. "But you definitely don't want to go in there. It's a stinking mess."

The captain offers Aunt Jackie a look that confirms my observation.

When I'm standing beside her again, I take the ukulele case and hug it to my chest. She puts her arm around my shoulders. I don't know everything about how I feel, or anything about how I should feel. I don't even really know how I want to feel. But I know without a doubt that the ground is solid beneath my feet and it feels good.